Volume V

All Right, Jack?

Frank English

2QT Limited (Publishing)

First Edition published 2019

2QT Limited (Publishing)
Settle, North Yorkshire
BD24 9BZ

Cover design: Charlotte Mouncey
Cover images: main photographs supplied by ©Frank English
Additional images from iStockhoto.com

Printed in Great Britain by IngramSparks UK Ltd

A CIP catalogue record for this book is available
from the British Library
ISBN 978-1-913071-27-1

To mi mam, Florence May English
Niver far away from mi mind and heart

Chapter 1

"Soon be under control, Mr Aston," the commanding voice of the Fire Chief cut into David's nightmare. First day of the glorious new academic year and … disaster!

It was bad enough the school taking such a catastrophic hit but losing a child and his great friend, Jack, was more than any sane person could bear.

"Is there any sign of one of our children and her teacher, Chief Oakenshore?" David said, hoping for at least some sort of news. "She sneaked out to the toilet, and he went after her with no thought for his own safety."

"No sign as yet, I'm afraid," the Chief went on, "but we still haven't been able to get near to the toilets. The flames are just about out, but the heat's much too intense. If anyone is still in there…"

A look of deep concern etched his craggy face as he shook his head slowly.

"But we'll keep on looking," he added. "Now, you'll have to excuse me. Hot spots to clear and men to direct."

"Any news, Mr Aston?" Jenny Smailes asked as he approached the frightened but silent group of teachers and children, some of whom were clearly upset at what they had just witnessed. "Mr Ingles? Cassie Pearson?"

The look on his face and the slow, almost imperceptible shaking of his head told his young Reception teacher all she feared to know.

"All we can do is hope and … pray," he added to his so far wordless response. In this case, words were a needless addition to an already dire and gloom-ridden situation.

Inevitable doubts began to crowd David's mind. If he hadn't brought Jack into *this* world he would still be alive. Alive? Why was he being so negative? How did he know for sure that Jack wasn't safe? What was he going to tell Jenny if the worst had happened? How could he even forgive *himself* and live with the consequences of this awful day?

He didn't need to ask why his friend had rushed back into school when he was safe with everyone else. *He* would have followed exactly the same path. He would have searched for Cassie Pearson without a second thought for his own safety. He knew *why* Jack wasn't here now having a rational conversation with him, but it didn't make him feel any better about his loss.

He couldn't get Jenny out of his mind. Losing her soul mate would destroy her. They had become inseparable, with neither able to function properly without the other – and her expecting their third child within a few months.

Loss? Why was he thinking like this, when nobody knew that he wasn't alive still, somewhere … close by – safe with Cassie. Now, *that's* what Jack would have done. He would have burst out of the danger area as soon as he realised what was about to happen. Better to be safe than sorry, *he* had always said, and…

"You need to come and see this, Dave," a gruff voice interrupted his thoughts, from behind.

David whisked around sharply, to see his good friend Terry, landlord of the Ship, turning on *his* heels, beckoning him to follow.

-o-

"I've had this feeling of disquiet growing on me all day,"

Jenny said to her mum as they sat in the new conservatory, with coffee and home-made scones Flo had brought.

"Disquiet?" Flo replied, a concerned frown drawing down her brow. "How do you mean?"

"Don't know, really," Jenny said slowly. "I've had these feelings several times before – when Dad died, for example, when Jessie's biological father was about to walk away from us, and when Val was having problems with William. Just something nagging away at the back of my mind."

"But, there's nothing could happen," Flo said, puzzled as to what might have brought this on. "Is there?"

"The only thing could be either Jessie's starting her new school," Jenny said after a moment or two of pondering, "or … Our Jack."

"If there had been anything wrong with Jessie," Flo suggested, "wouldn't they have let you know by now?"

"Then, Jack," Jenny replied. "It has to be Jack. Though I have no idea what he's…"

The telephone's insistent and insidious warble interrupted her. Mother and daughter stiffened visibly, casting fearful glances at each other as the machine urged either one or the other to pick it up.

-o-

"Where is he? What's happened?" Jenny's tremulous voice cut through the noise of fire engines and the intermittent strobing of emergency lights. "David?"

Flo Arkwright closed the car door as Jenny lurched towards the charred and smoky remains of the school's entrance, cloakrooms and toilets. The last child was being ushered into her mum's car, to be whisked away from this scene of devastation. The school was uninhabitable and would remain so for the foreseeable future.

"Jenny," David said, sliding his arm around her

shoulders and drawing her heaving frame to him.

"Where … is … he?" she replied, as deep sobs convulsed her already heaving shoulders. "I must see him. Is he hurt? Is he…?"

"Come with me," he urged quietly as he led her unresisting body towards the Ship Inn where, by now, the whole teaching staff had gathered. It was almost noon and the Ship had been closed to all save those involved with the catastrophic events of only a few short hours previously. Wispy streamers of steam spiralling from large catering pots of hot tea and coffee dominated the bar area, with staff consuming sandwiches as well, made for them by Terry and his wife Rebecca.

"What you have to remember, Jenny," David started to explain quietly without letting her go, "is that, without Jack, one little girl wouldn't be sitting down to tea tonight."

Jenny's head lolled onto his shoulder. She was resigned to hearing the worst, until she caught sight of a form she recognised instantly, hand bandaged and jacketless, in the corner by the bar. She let out a piercing screech and, wrenching away from David's supportive grasp, she launched herself across the room. With eyes streaming and breath escaping in relieved gasps, she gathered this man to her heaving bosom.

"Jack! Jack!" she sobbed. "I thought I'd lost you."

"I wasn't so sure missen either, Our Jen," Jack sighed, once she had finished covering him in relieved kisses. "It was touch and go at one stage, I can tell you, and I didn't think we were off to mek it. I went after a little girl who I knew would catch it…"

His voice trailed away into the general relieved murmurs and smoke-related coughing and wheezing, coming from most of those present. Low-level muttering spluttered around the room, interrupted periodically by food-induced quiet.

"…Bloody 'ero, yon 'usband o' yours, Missus," the deeply urgent voice of the Chief Fire Officer rumbled back in, setting to vibrate his thick, grey walrus moustache that covered almost the whole of his mouth.

"Aye! Rayt!" Jack interrupted sceptically. "All I did was to follow mi nose automatically. Training, you see, and—"

"Aye, but thi trainin' dint tell thi to put thi own life in danger to save another," the Fire Chief interrupted. "*That* were *instinct*, and, I don't usually say this but, it's a rayt good job it did, otherwise one little lass wouldn't be 'ere now. We were onny just getting' 'ere and settin' up as yon entrance erupted. So, don't minimise what tha did, young man."

All the time he had been talking, Jenny had kept a tight hold on her man as her tears flowed. To think, saving another's life, could have cost his own, and that would have been unbearable.

"Mr Ingles? Where's Mr Ingles?" an emotional female voice erupted into the room, a little girl in tow.

Jack heaved himself to his feet slowly, to greet his next verbal assailant, only to be drawn into a desperate hug he wouldn't easily escape.

"Wi' out you," the woman said, voice quavering with emotion as tears welled and flooded her cheeks, "my little Cassie wouldn't be 'ere … and she's all I've got. I can't thank you enough for savin' mi little treasure."

She hung of for as long as she felt was right and seemly, and then, releasing him abruptly, she spun on her heels and led her Cassie through the throng, and disappeared.

"Well," Jenny whispered as she reclaimed his clammy hand, "another grateful fan. Thank goodness she was *able* to thank you in person."

"My God!" David sighed deeply as he dropped in to the bench seat next to his friend and sliding his arm around his broad shoulders. "Am I glad you're still here."

"Not going to get rid of me *that* easily, Old Chap," Jack smiled ruefully as he held his bandaged hand close to his chest. "You'd have to re-interview."

"It's all ower, Mr Aston," Fire Chief Oakenshore urged, "but nobody is to enter the building for at least forty-eight hours. We've put prohibition notices and 'DO NOT ENTER' tapes around the entrance. So, now we'll be off. Good luck."

"What do we do now then, Boss?" Jack said quietly to David.

"We get you home straight away, my boy," David insisted. "You've done enough today if you never do another thing in this school. So, your beautiful wife is now going to take you home and keep you away until I telephone you tell you it's safe to return. OK?"

"Yes, oh worshipful one," Jack replied, regaining some of his old humour. "To hear is to … obey."

"Don't run away with the idea that you're anything special," David laughed. "Everyone else is going home, too."

"Thanks, mate," Jack replied, a grin emerging. "I love you too, but don't tell anyone else. They'll think I've gone soft."

-o-

"Jack!" Jenny's mum exclaimed in horror as he slid into Jim's Rover 95 leather seats. "Your hand? What have you done?"

Town Street passed leisurely by as Jack launched into his tale of how the first day at his new school almost ended in catastrophe. This tale took Jim Arkwright back to *his* first shift down a little-known colliery near Castleford. A conveyor, trundling coal to the bottom of the shaft ready for extraction, collapsed and sparked, igniting a fortunately small pocket of fire damp, scorching his hair and arms. *That* was a frightening experience he had no wish to replay but made him understand how Jack must have felt.

"...And as we couldn't get past the toilet door," Jack's voice faded in, "I covered little Cassie with my jacket, smashed through the window – hence the bandage – and, pushing her terrified little body out first, we escaped just as the front of the building went up. We managed to stumble across to where the old building was, where Terry from the Ship found us and ushered us very rapidly into *his* place."

"My goodness," Flo gasped incredulously, "and how was it that such a thing could happen with a new school?"

"Bad design, I suppose," Jack said, shrugging and settling back at last. "Kitchen next to the cloakrooms and toilets? I mean…"

"Asking for trouble," Jenny joined in, drawing her Jack even closer. "Hero, Mum. That's our Jack. Fire Chief said so."

"Nay. Gi ower," Jack interrupted, closing his eyes with a sigh. "I onny did what I thowt were rayt, like any other right-thinking human being."

"Ah," Jenny went on, "but it wasn't a case of being right-thinking, was it? Like Fire Chief Oakenshore said, it was instinct that drove you to save that little girl, and that's what brought you through, thank goodness."

All the while, little Flo snoozed in the back in her comfortable toddler seat, oblivious to the drama unfolding around her. They would collect her sister in a few moments from *her* first day at her new school, without sharing this news with her. That sort of excitement she didn't need, on top of what she had probably done during this day. No doubt she would be ready for her nap, too.

"Another few days off then, Our Jack," Jenny's mum said, a smile supporting her happiness that these youngsters could have a bit more quality time together.

"Perhaps a good moment to tell you our little secret, then, Mum," Jenny said, once they had reached Moortown.

"What," Flo replied quickly, "that you are pregnant?"

"We should have known better than to think we could keep that from you, Our Flo," Jack said, suppressing a hearty laugh so as not to wake little Flo.

"Don't forget, Jack," Flo went on, a smile curling the corners of her mouth, "I've had two of my own, and, however intuitive, psychic and mystical my Jenny might think she is, she still has a lot to learn from her mother."

"Well," Jenny replied, one eyebrow raised and her head cocked slightly to the other side, in that disbelievingly quizzical way, "it was either an amazingly good shot, or she has divine insight that none of *us* understands."

-o-

"Mammy! Mammy!" Jessie yelled, as Grandpa Jim's car drew to a halt outside the main gates of her school. She stopped twinding the long skipping rope with her new friends and rushed to the gate. "Come watch me skipping with Joanie and Jeanie. They're twins."

Jenny walked towards the playground, hardly able to believe the confident young lady she had become, doing things she wouldn't have attempted only a few short months ago.

"Are Nana and Grandpa Arkerite and Daddy in the car?" she asked, finding it difficult to pronounce their name. "Do they want to come and…"

"It's all right, my poppet," Jenny replied, "they can see from there. Show *me*."

"That's excellent, my rope-twirling demon!" Jack shouted as he joined his wife by the gate. "Much less of a 'little' girl now, Our Jen. Don't you think?"

Jenny found it hard to answer because of the little

lump of pride fighting with deeper emotions in her throat. A tear glistened and threatened to open flood gates if they continued with this conversation. Recognising her difficulty, Jack slid his arm around her shoulders, and beckoned for his daughter to join them.

"Why have you got a bandage on your hand, Our Daddy Jack?" Jessie asked as she threw her little arms about his waist.

"It's not a bandage," he answered quickly. "It's a glove, because my hand is cold. I've always wanted a pair of white gloves."

"Then, why do you have only one?" Jessie's words came back at him quickly. "And why have you no fingers in that glove? Why is your other hand bare?"

"Bare?" he said, making her laugh as he made a big show of searching his pockets and inside his jumper. "Bare? Oh dear, no! Someone's stolen my other glove. Where's my other white glove? I had it a moment or two ago."

"Silly Daddy," Jessie laughed. "I don't see your jacket either. Did someone steal that too?"

Jenny and her mum burst out laughing at the sharply pert answer that flew out of Jessie's mind. My, she was a quick one that Jessie, jerking Jack's mind back to clear focus as to why he was still alive. In this one close-knit group beat the heart of his existence – the reason he needed not to become too introspective or mildly cavalier in his view of the world at large. Here was his reason to rejoice in the life his mam had given him and had nurtured almost to the time he became independent. This he owed and dedicated to her.

Jim and Flo cast each other a knowing glance. This man could bring the sun out on the most dire and dreadful scene, telling everyone what was important in their lives.

All right, Jack!

Chapter 2

"I've been on to the Fire Chief," David's voice crackled around the telephone's Bakelite receiver, "and he reckons it's safe enough for us to enter school by the side door. So, I was wondering—"

"If you and I could nip into school and assess?" Jack interrupted with a smile.

"Two o'clock this afternoon, do you?" David replied.

"You mean you want to drag me away from my beautiful family's extra holiday," Jack laughed, "to spend the day in school?"

"What better way to spend half a day?" David quipped, his usual ebullient personality taking over.

"Everything OK?" Jenny asked, as Jack released the handset back to its cradle.

"Holiday's over I'm afraid," he replied, a pretend look of sadness covering his face. "We knew it would have to end some time soon, but I was hoping…"

"So?" she asked, seeing as he wasn't about to explain.

"This aft, at two," Jack said, "just to look around the school to see what has to and can be done to get folks back in. We can't stay closed forever."

"I don't think I've ever been in one of your schools, Our Jack," Jenny said. "Do you mind if I tag along, as long as we're not too late back?"

"I'd be honoured, Milady," he replied, bowing low with

an exaggerated medieval flourish of his arm.

-o-

"It's quarter to two," David said quietly to the disparate group milling around him, "and if I know him, he'll be here before his due time. He'd rather be twenty minutes early than one minute late, which means we have to be on our mettle if this is to work. And don't lose sight of the fact that he's intellectually very sharp – painfully so sometimes. This will mean, of course, that he'll know instinctively if there's anything amiss if *you* are not at the top of *your* game, because he's always at the top of *his*."

"So, what would you like us to do?" one pretty young woman asked.

"Do your *thing*," David replied slowly, emphasising his last word deliberately, "and keep out of sight until I give the nod."

The acrid stench of smoke and melted plastic pervaded, lurking around every conceivable corner and in rooms that had remained locked throughout. Even the outer recesses of the school furthest from the fire bore its signature smell, carried through the hidden cavities of the false ceiling. The totally open-plan all-class teaching idea, based on a Scandinavian concept, heralded new significant, insidious and silent dangers. This new-wave learning idea, however, hadn't been thought-through seriously, with its inherent problems, casting doubt in parents' minds as to the safety their bairns *should* be enjoying.

"*They're* new," Jack said as they got out of the car, pointing to eight terrapin mobile classrooms, that seemed to have sprouted from where the old school used to be. "I wonder why—?"

"Jack! Jenny!" David's voice interrupted his pal's thoughts as he hugged his friends. "Good to see you both. You've seen our new school then?"

"New…?" Jack stammered, not really taking in what David was telling him.

"We can't use the real school for a few months," David began to explain. "therefore, the Authority delivered these classroom units yesterday, so we can maintain some semblance of normality. We can use the bottom playground as usual, but each of the six units is large enough for one class of children at a time only."

As they approached the main entrance, barriers and a huge smack-in-the-face red sign hinted at the dire repercussions should they not heed its warning not to pass.

"Wow," Jack whistled at the devastation he now witnessed. "No brass bands and ribbons today. Side door it is, then."

"It'll take more than a few months to get rid of that eye-watering smell," Jenny said as they trod the side door's threshold. "Try fumigation and a few gallons of Chanel number 5."

"Excuse me. Mr Ingles?" a light female voice asked as a figure stepped out from behind a wide partition. "Mr *Jack* Ingles?"

Jack swung round sharply, to see a pretty young lady in a smart straight-skirted suit, permed hair style, and high-heeled red shoes, a small note pad and pencil to hand.

"Jessie Hawes, Evening Post. May I ask you about the day of the fire?" she went on, her voice fading gradually away as she opened her note pad and made ready to take notes.

The words 'Mr *Jack* Ingles' seemed to be a signal for other people to appear, magically, from nooks and corners of this almost cornerless hangar of a building. Screens and cupboards had provided most of the hiding places for individuals and small groups alike.

One of the first to make a purposeful bee-line for what seemed to be everyone's focus of attention, was

Cassie Pearson's mum, with her daughter very much in tow. Within moments a crowd had gathered, with Jack as its nucleus. Each member of that group wanted a piece of him as Jenny and David backed quietly and surreptitiously away, smiles lingering around satisfied mouth corners.

Once newspaper, radio, television and local dignitaries had had their fill, and many photographs had been taken, the room gradually emptied as Jack surfaced from the scrum, a mixed look of relief, shock and elation, enlightening his face.

"What just happened?" he said, exhaling as he staggered to join his wife and his pal. "You had something to do with this, didn't you, Mr Aston?"

"Well…" David hesitated.

"We both did," Jenny interrupted quickly.

"What on earth for?" Jack asked, a frown flicking across his face.

"Because it was the right thing to do," Jenny insisted. "Don't you realise that what you did saved that little girl's life? Don't you dare dismiss it. It was – is – a big deal, so you'd better get used to the adulation you are about to receive, Buster."

"Well said, Our Jenny," David added. "False modesty just doesn't cut it, Jack. These people won't let you – or anyone else – forget what you did. Enjoy it while it's there. Our very own Super Hero."

-o-

"Well, that was a caution, and no mistake, and you knew? You never let on," Jack sighed on the way home.

"Why would I?" she replied, kissing his cheek and smiling broadly in a huge flush of pride. "This is *your* moment, my lovely man."

"Hadn't we better hurry to pick up our two?" he went on.

"No need," Jenny replied with a self-satisfied smile. "Mum and Jim have it under control."

"The plot thickens," Jack said, not quite sufficiently under his breath. "How could you have organised all this and me not know? Are you training to be a spy?"

Jenny laughed as they turned on to King Lane for the last green mile to their home and family. Autumn was already beginning to make its presence felt early, with brown and yellow leaves and sycamore helicopters, borne on a chill breeze, filling the air. The warm Indian summers that took over early autumn when Jack was a nipper, now were fewer and further between. How he loved that time, between the beginning of September and early October. Now *that* was his most favourite time of year, after spring and winter. He most definitely wasn't a lover of the hot summers they had been used to having, year on year.

It had always been a nuisance, as a youngster to have to take a big empty dandelion and burdock glass pop bottle, that he had filled with cold water from home when he traipsed into the fields with his mates on a hot summer's day. Many's the time he'd called at someone's house, after he had supped the bottle's contents, over Goosehill and Newlands way, to ask if they might fill his empty bottle with cold water for him. They always did.

There had been a row of little cottages just ower yon railway bridge on the way to the colliery close by, and the folks at the first house never failed him.

It wor like gold wor that bottle, and he had to guard it and its contents wi' his life. He wouldn't let any of his mates drink out on it, not wi' their slaver and spit around its neck.

"Gi us a sup o' thi watter," Gordon Gittins would say.

"Bugger off!" Jack would reply. "Bring thi own."

"Don't be so bloomin' tight," Gordon Gittins would say.

"Don't be so bloomin' idle," Jack would retort. "Fetch thi own. Tha's 'avin' none o' mine."

He remembered the year – 1957 it was – when Mr Tomlinson, his headteacher at Woodhouse, had brought the news to his mam that he had passed his scholarship for the Grammar School. Whitsuntide holiday. Jack was in the front garden, playing on the lawn, when Mr Tomlinson clicked the front gate. Jack had sprung to attention almost at the mere sight of his dapper, suited frame. He lived down Cambridge Street way on, did Mr Tomlinson. Not far from Mr Chivers, deputy headteacher from another junior school in Normanton. Jack remembered going out as a seventeen-year-old briefly with *his* daughter, Janet.

She was lovely, was Janet, but rugby-playing lads of Jack's age usually concentrated on one thing only, and *that* wasn't courting.

1957's summer was a hot one, but then, weren't they all? It was difficult to accept that, ten years down the line, his mam would be with him no longer. That was a hard one to swallow, and one upon which he dare not dwell. It didn't seem fair that such a good, inoffensive person should have lived only fifty-three years and not seen her sons grow up to become good people, too.

He missed his mam and that strong close bond they had allus shared. He recalled those cold winter evenings when she sat in the rocking chair by the kitchen living room fire, crocheting, and he sat on the floor by her knees. When he was little she would often stop for a while to stroke his spiky hair, as he stared into the flames imagining the monsters the hot coals formed before his eyes.

"Well," Jenny said as she pulled into their driveway, "I don't know where you've been for the last while, but…"

"I've bin wi' mi mam," he replied quietly, almost apologetically, "sitting by yon kitchen fire in Garth Avenue."

"I'm sorry love," she said quietly. "I didn't mean to…"

"Don't be so daft," he grinned. "My thoughts are your thoughts, anyway. You should know that. Now for them there bairns, and a big 'Thank you' to Flo and Jim for being there."

-o-

"Do you realise what would have happened if the fire had broken out only ten minutes earlier?" Jack said after they had put the young 'uns to bed and were sitting in front of the glowing embers of their log fire. "I can't get that awful thought out of my head."

"I know," Jenny said quietly, trying to soothe away his hurt as she shifted uncomfortably on the sofa.

"Yon bairn causing you grief, Our Jen?" Jack asked, moving over to put his arm around her shoulders.

"Just a bit," she sighed, leaning on his broad accommodating shoulder. "Two months down and another seven to go."

"So that would make his appearance around about April time?" he added, a thoughtful furrow deepening his brow.

"*His* appearance?" she smiled. "Do you know something I don't?"

"I just have this … feeling," he said slowly.

"Aye," she laughed. "That 'feeling' was the start of all this."

Jack settled back, drew his lovely close to him, and let out a hearty guffaw at the thought.

"I could share another feeling if you want?" he said, winking and giggling.

"Not just now, thank you very much," she chuckled. "You'll have to wait your rush."

"Will three be enough for you, then?" he asked, a proud smile developing. "Or, would you like some more?

Perhaps another two?"

"I think three might be just about do," she said, a smile verging on a grimace supporting her words, "especially ifn yon newby is the boy you're banking on."

"And if he's a *she?*" Jack laughed.

"I think three's enough," she reiterated, quietly but decisively, her final nod drawing an invisible line under the discussion.

"That fire couldn't have happened in the old school, of course," Jack said after a few moments' silent thought.

"How do you mean?" Jenny asked.

"Unfortunately, this *new* building smells more like a glorified open canteen than a school," Jack explained, wrinkling his nose to show his distaste. "Cooking lunch usually starts about half ten, and the odours of cooked food linger well into the afternoon."

"That shouldn't be a problem for you, my lovely walking dustbin," Jenny replied, an infectious grin spreading across her face.

"Don't get me wrong," he said, grinning at the thought. "I love mi vittels, as you so evidently point out. I just don't like to smell it before *and* after the event – especially in school."

"You don't *have* to go into lunch, do you?" she puzzled. Easy answer to an even easier question.

"It's not that easy, my lovely," he went on slowly, as he stared into the bottom of a near-empty tea mug. "You have to remember that there is no separate dining facility here. Nothing."

"Sorry?" she butted in. "How do you mean? Nothing as in they can eat, but there's nowhere to eat it?"

"Almost," he grimaced. "Food is brought in from the kitchens on several heated trolleys, and served to the kids at their learning tables, where they consume it among their books and pencils and stuff. Imagine the mess where they will be doing their work shortly afterwards."

"Yuk!" Jenny added, almost vomiting at the thought. "You mean to say they…?"

"A team of cleaners comes in after the gravy fight, de-sticks the tables and cleans away the debris," Jack said. "But, it's not good."

"What's going to happen for the next month or two," Jenny asked, "while you're in temporary classrooms?"

"Well," he began slowly, gathering his thoughts as he spoke, "as far as I am aware – and contrary to the popular belief that I am the fount of all knowledge—"

"Yeah! Right!" she scoffed.

"David tells me," he went on, "that of the eight mobile classrooms we have been given, six will be class bases, one will be a staff area, and the other a dining room, where food will be brought in from a central kitchen."

"Wow," she said, whistling softly at the logistics of it all.

"The funny thing is," he smiled, "that the person organising it all is no other than Mrs Dyer, our excellent cook from the old school, who moved to take up some senior position with the Schools' Catering Division before I left Broughton yonks ago. Silver lining, eh?"

"Containerised, second-hand, luke-warm food?" she grimaced. "Not sure."

"It won't be like yours," Jack said as he drew her to him, "but I won't be eating it."

"How—?" she stammered. She couldn't for the life of her see her Jack not eating throughout the day.

"Don't worry," he laughed. "I'll be taking sandwiches. Corned beef every day. Bliss."

The warble of the telephone interrupted the look of joy on his face at the thought of his favourite snack.

"I'll get it," Jenny offered as she edged from the sofa, and on her way to the hall. "Going to put the kettle on anyway."

"I keep telling you it won't suit you at all," Jack quipped, receiving no response, because *that* retort was one of his standards. It *was* funny if you'd never heard it before. It was one of his granddad's, after all, and he felt honour and duty-bound to keep *his* funnies alive – for posterity.

"Problem?" Jack asked as his wife settled down again beside him, a look of concern clouding her eyes.

"It was Val," she replied, not quite knowing what to say as she slowed to a halt.

"And?" he urged, with that puzzled frown stitching his brows together. "Now what's he done?"

Chapter 3

"Come on then," Jack urged his wife, "spill the beans. What's Our William been up to now? Another floosie?"

"To be honest," she replied, "I don't know. Our Val has said only that she wanted to talk, so she'll be around in about half an hour. It's not as if she's hours away and will want to stay over – and it's only early."

"Hey," he said, with a non-committal raising of the eyebrows, "it's no skin off my nose when she comes and how long she stays. I'm not back in school until Monday, so whatever needs thrashing out can be well and truly thrashed, however long it takes. I suppose William will be staying with the kids?"

"Presumably," Jenny replied, a look of uncertainty hovering. "I can't read her these days. She seems to have become more … introspective, almost more introverted than she ever used to be. Fighting with something she's determined to overcome but not quite there."

"'Ark at you," he laughed. "Jenny Freud. If ever I need psychoanalysing…"

Jenny smiled. She could always rely on Jack to make her smile and take her mind away from the worrying issues in her life. You always knew where you stood with him and could always expect to get a straight answer. Straight forward and honest almost to the point of rudeness. She wouldn't have him any other way. He was like a curved room – no corners to hide behind.

"I'll get it," Jack said, leaping to his feet on hearing the doorbell. "It'll be Val."

Jenny cocked her ear to try to make out the mutterings but knew the score straight away when she heard Jack's clear 'Stand by to repel boarders', as the whole family trouped through into the lounge.

"I knew you wouldn't be able to stay away for long," Jack said to Joey and Ed, drawing a smile to their face.

"Needs must, Uncle Jack," Joey replied. "So, I don't want you to get your hopes up."

Jack let out a hearty guffaw as he brought in a tray bearing cups, tea pot, cafetiere and baked goodies, along with milk and orange juice to follow for the youngsters.

"We won't be staying long," Val promised, "but there is a couple of issues William and I would like to run past you, if that's all right."

"Fire away," Jack said as he chomped on his spice cake and warmed his hands around his mug of tea.

The youngsters had taken themselves off to the conservatory, and so would not be party to any discussion or decisions taken.

"Lovely cake," William said through a mouthful.

"Yes, but that's not what we came to talk about," Val added sharply, giving him one of her withering looks.

"Let me guess," Jack butted in. "School and Savanah?"

"Samantha," Jenny corrected. "She was called Samantha."

"How did you guess that, Jack?" Val gasped. "We have come to accept you as the fount of all knowledge, but that…?"

"Stands to sense," Jack answered, "that the only two things in recent history worthy of a family pow wow have been school and Our William's floosie."

"Jack!" Jenny interrupted, hoping to stop him from developing that line any further.

"Just saying," he offered with a non-committal shrug. "So, what's happened on the 'other woman' front, then, William?"

"Her husband found out about her many affairs and divorced her," he said quietly. "Came round to see me."

"To knock your block off?" Jack laughed.

"Actually, no," William added. "Of all things, to thank me."

"To thank…?" Jenny and Jack chorused. "How…?"

"For some reason, he reckoned had it not been for my involvement," William went on with a puzzled shrug, "he wouldn't have found out about all the others."

"And how did she take *that*?" Jenny asked, a look of shock showing her feelings.

"She tried to reel him in again," Val said brusquely, "with promises of goodness knows what tasty tit bits. I soon gave her short shrift. She won't be back after what I said to her."

"And school?" Jack piled in quickly. "I thought everything was settled for both of you?"

"It is," William added, "but not how you might think."

"Go on then," Jack sighed. "Shock me."

"The school I'm at now," his brother started, "has fallen through."

"Fallen through?" Jack said, a deeply puzzled frown invading his face. "But … you're there, aren't you?"

"The contract was – is – only a temporary one," William replied, "subject to certain conditions, the most important of which turned out to be stable children numbers and … continued finance."

"But, wasn't that a given when you took the job?" Jack puzzled, still not sure where this was going.

"Special circumstances," William said, which, with

hindsight, meant absolutely … nothing.

"Wow," Jack sighed, his surprise tangible. "No job – again – then?"

"Well," William said with a sardonic smile, "not exactly."

"Come on you owd dark horse," Jack interrupted. "There's more to thee than meets the eye sometimes, si thi. Spill."

"Can't keep anything from you, Our Jack," Val laughed. "I told William you'd see through it."

"You've got another job, haven't you," Jack said. Touching the side of his nose with his fore finger. "One of those 'others' you had in abeyance, I'll be bound."

"Hole in one, Old Chap," his brother agreed. "I get paid at my present school until Christmas, and then start the new school in January as … deputy head of a largish junior school – wait for it – down Castleford Road in Normanton."

"You jammy…" Jack guffawed. "'Fallen' and 'feet' spring to mind, eh?"

"And," William continued, "the head isn't far from retirement either. Things beginning to look up, eh? But, that's not the best of it."

"Meaning?" Jenny asked, stumped by his cryptic response. "There's more?"

"The deputy at *my* school," Val chipped in, "has gone off on indefinite sick leave, and…"

"Don't tell me that they've asked you to take over?" Jack said, heaving a deep, resigned sigh.

"Temporarily for a couple of terms," Val replied, "until they've had time to rethink what they need to do. The only problem is, I won't be able to pick up Mary and the boys after school – no car because of Will's job in the old town."

"Not a problem, big sister," Jenny butted in. "Mary

goes to the same school as Jessie, so I can pick them all up, and they can stay here until you get back. We can arrive at a reasonable rate for the job."

"That's ma girl," Jack guffawed, followed by his brother and sister-in-law.

"But what about Jack?" Val pointed out. "Won't he need the car?"

I always travel by big green Atlantean," Jack replied.

"Atl…?" Val puzzled.

"Corporation bus," Jenny said, laughing at their ignorance. "When was the last time *you* used public transport?"

"Anyway," William asked, "couldn't you get a lift with that friend of yours? Stick, isn't it?"

"We often travel together on the bus," Jack explained. "Joyce is expecting – due about the same time as us, so she has the car."

"How's that going then sis?" Val asked as they went to the kitchen to put the kettle on again. "Has it been…?"

Their voices faded away as the door snecked behind them, leaving a gentle soft hum of controlled conversation in both conservatory and lounge, in due deference to their sleeping beauties upstairs.

"So, we'd like you all to come to ours this Christmas," Val's voice drifted back in. "Boxing Day as well. There are one or two new recipes I'd like to try out on you. "

"And you and William?" Jenny asked pointedly. "How are things? Jogging along?"

"Just that," she replied with a sigh. "Moving forward but very slowly, I'm afraid. I think we've lost what we had, irreplaceably, and I suppose it's about building something new, something that's not as good as … what attracted us to each other in the first place. Can I do it? I honestly don't know, Jen."

"Don't we all go through periods of change, though,"

Jenny replied, "throughout our lives together? I mean…"

"Not in such a short space of time," Val replied, a look of disappointment and resignation creeping in. "It's what an affair does to a relationship, I fully appreciate. However. Can I cope and put it behind me? Only time will tell."

"That tea and cake ready yet?" Jack's voice shouldered its way into the room.

"Now," Val laughed, "*that* one will *never* change. You'll always know where you are with him. Lucky you."

"What did I miss?" he said as he squeezed round the door. "I know what I missed – my tea and cake."

He sucked in his cheeks, rolled his eyes, and staggered around as if he was fainting from lack of food, which made the sisters laugh out loud.

"All right, all right," Jenny said, a giggle still resting in her throat, "point taken. Get thissen back into yon lounge and we'll bring it through."

"Thissen? Yon?" Val puzzled. "You never used to speak like that, Our Jen."

"And you never used to say 'Our Jen', either," her sister replied. "Comes with living with a true red-blooded Yorkshireman, I suppose."

–o–

"Not long to go to the great day, eh Jack?" a voice he recognised crept up on him in the bus queue, Monday morning.

"Do you mean retirement day, or the return of the Great Redeemer?" he replied, turning slowly. "I'd recognise that voice anywhere, John Walker."

"Not looking that far afield on both counts," Stick laughed. "You always were an idealist, Jack Ingles."

"Good weekend?" Jack asked.

"In all honesty, I should have to say no," Stick sighed. "Joyce hasn't been too good, you know. Morning sickness that she didn't experience with Our Valerie. I could do without turning in today, really, but she insisted. Even threatened she might throw up on me if I didn't go. So how could I resist *that* sort of an offer?"

The bus was almost full with regulars by the time it reached their getting-on stop, and so, knowing which older women would be likely to catch the bus next, they both stood in the gangway. The new-fangled service buses were all driver-only operated, giving them opportunity to buy cheaper multi-ticket strips that had to be automatic machine-cancelled on the bus. More efficient, the bus company said – cheaper to run without a conductor everyone else said.

"Bad do with the fire at your place, Jack," Stick said once they could guarantee nobody else would be trying to push past them for at least the next ten minutes. "Anybody hurt?"

"Only the Chief Education Officer's wallet," Jack said, a definite grin lighting up his face.

"And it appears I'm standing by the shoulder of a god," Stick went on, slapping Jack on the back.

"But only a minor one," Jack said, trying to make light.

"Ey, Jack," Stick replied earnestly, "don't make light on it. Everybody in this area now knows who Jack Ingles is, and what he did for one of theirs. They won't ever forget."

"Infamy! Infamy!" Jack replied.

"They've all got it in for me!" Stick joined in as they laughed together.

Their conversation about Broughton's financial demise filled the rest of their journey to town and then on to school, until they reached Old Lane where John got off to trudge his way to work.

The temporary classrooms, as Jack strode past the bus terminus, once again brought home the near-miss all his children had had only a week before. This was a

Scarborough Warning none of them would be able to ignore – ever – particularly if Jack Ingles had anything to do with it. At least they would be able to eat in relative peace, untroubled by pervading aromas in the afternoon of what they had eaten for lunch.

"Good morning, folks," he said, as he announced that Jack Ingles had entered the building.

"Good morning, Jack," David's breezy answer greeted him. "How's Krypton today?"

"Ha bloomin' ha!" Jack replied, batting the greeting back at him. "Any sign of Cassie Pearson this morning?"

"Not seen her yet," David replied, "but her mum said, despite being upset at what happened, she *will* be here. Can we go into my office? There's something I want you to know."

"Office?" Jack puzzled. "There isn't a mobile classroom for…"

Looking around this new staffroom, he noticed a closed door at the end of the room.

Jack finished his observation, realising that *that* door hid…

"Your temporary office," he said, "is behind that door, isn't it?"

"Very observant, Old Chap," David agreed, smiling at his little trick.

"This is all right, mon capitaine," Jack whistled as the door to David's new office clicked behind him. "Perhaps we ought to pull the school down, put a playground in its place, and stay down here."

"Don't imagine for a minute I haven't thought of that one," David said, heaving a huge sigh. "Its design has given us a few logistical nightmares, I can tell you. For goodness' sake, which school can function without a proper hall and dining area, eh? Tell me that one."

"To be serious though," Jack replied, sympathising

with his dilemma, "if they're not going to allow us to keep any of these giant pill boxes, why not build onto the side of yon, put the kitchens in it along with an eating place, and turn the present kitchen into a hall?"

"I can always rely on you to hit-nail-on-head, Our Jack," David said, an enormous grin lighting his face. "That's exactly what *I* had in mind."

"It can't be difficult, surely," Jack added. "The school's made out of cardboard anyway. Badly and cheaply designed, but quite easy to remedy, I should think."

"And how would you go about it?" David asked, an earnest look covering his face.

"Build the extension with double the floor space where the present kitchens are for an assembly hall-cum-dining space, shift the kitchen stuff into the new area, boom boom. Job's a good un," Jack said, a look of satisfaction settling. "Back in by October half-term."

"I've a meeting with the Chief Planning Officer, here after school tomorrow," David said. "I should like you to be in on it. Any chance?"

"Of course there is, David," Jack agreed. "You know me. Any chance to put in my ha'p'orth, I'm your man."

-o-

"Wow!" Jenny gasped when Jack told her about the school alterations to be finished before Christmas. "And they accepted *everything* you suggested?"

"Well," he added as he sipped his Saturday mid-morning tea and nibbled his accompanying chocolate digestive biscuit, "David did have a bit of a hand in it, too, you know. He told me yesterday that our suggestions had gone through on the nod, and building would start very soon."

"That's amazing," she replied, "but how…?"

"Actually, I think they got wind of mi new status in

Broughton," he grinned.

"New status?" she asked, slightly puzzled at the reference.

"The Caped Crusader?" he hinted. "The man whom everyone knows and listens to?"

"Get you," she said, bursting into giggles. "My superman. So, apart from influencing important decisions and standing up for the folks of that area, how did your week go?"

Their conversation faded out to the joyous squeals of Jessie and Florence May as they sat in the conservatory watching flurries of snow floating by and collecting slowly on surfaces, as they tried to change all colours to white.

Chapter 4

"You're not going to believe this," Jack said through a stifled yawn as he sneaked a peek through a chink in the bedroom curtains.

"What am I not going to believe?" Jenny's muffled voice crawled out from under her bed covers. The central heating boiler's beat thrummed reassuringly in the background as the rooms warmed to Jenny's acceptable level for her to venture from her bed into the inhospitable morning air.

"The sun's shining from a gloriously blue sky," he replied slowly, trying to excite her to make a move towards breakfast.

"Really?" she said, a surprised catch in her throat as the top of her head emerged.

"Actually, no," he said, suppressing a rising giggle. "There are at least four inches of snow, and it's still coming down."

"Are you telling the truth?" she said, unsure as to what she should believe.

"Of course I am," he assured her. "When have you ever known me not to tell the truth?"

"Ah, but which one is the truth?" she said accusingly, her head finally in the real world as Jessie yawned her way through their bedroom doorway, flopping onto their bed and snuggling up to her mammy. "Time, Jack?"

"I have the time but you don't have the inclination, my sweet one," he laughed. "Just off to make breakfast. Anything in particular you'd like?"

"Usual, please," she said, sliding out from underneath her still snoozing daughter.

"Would that be toast and smoked salmon with a nice cup of elegant Yorkshire Tea?" he said, laughing all the way to the foot of the stairs.

"Daft bugger," she muttered as she shuffled into their en suite bathroom.

"That would be a no, then?" he said, carrying on laughing on his way to making his world famous and renowned breakfast of porridge and fruit.

"Well," he muttered, looking out at the snow, "first day of the Christmas holidays and this has to happen."

"Not keen on snow, then, my lovely?" Jenny asked from just behind him, making him jump.

"Nervous I'm going to make you go out to build a snowman or an igloo for your children?" she laughed, as he turned towards her, a look of mischievous warning in his eyes.

"I'll get you back for that," he warned with a grin. "Just you wait and see, when you are least expecting it. I can wait."

-o-

"And who was it agreed to visit William's new school," Jenny asked after breakfast, "and to spend a couple of hours in All Saints' cemetery in Normanton tending graves?"

"All right. All right," Jack agreed. "Not such a good idea perhaps, but I didn't know it was about to snow on the day we chose. We can cancel and go another day, can't we? We…"

The jangling sound of an insistent doorbell stopped him in his tracks, as an annoyed frown sprang to his face.

"And *that* would be the reason we won't be cancelling," Jenny said, as she moved to the front door.

Occasionally Jack was slow on the uptake, as Jenny would often like to remind him. He should have known that she would have made arrangements for her children to be looked after, so they didn't have to traipse out in the cold. What she didn't know was that Val's youngsters wouldn't want to go out either. So…

"Flo! Jim!" Jack exclaimed as they trouped into the lounge with William and his brood in happy tow. "My goodness! Are you going to tame this motley crew for the time we'll be escaping?"

"Joey and Ed have homework to do," Val said, "and we have agreed they will do it straight away, rather than having it as a Sword of Damocles hanging over them until the last day."

"Has Mary got homework as well?" Jack said, keeping the laughter he wanted to share under control.

"No, Uncle Jack," Mary interrupted. "I have my dolls and toys and books enough to keep *me* occupied, thank you very much. Not so sure how much work my brothers will get done either."

Jack could contain his mirth no longer at Mary's adult stance. Those sorts of pert answers you didn't expect from a child of her age, in those sorts of terms. A seven-year-old going on thirty-seven.

"Are you sure you're going to be all right, Mum?" Jenny asked, ever mindful that Jim and her weren't getting any younger, and how much of a handful youngsters could be.

"Of course we are, silly," she replied, a benign smile on her face. "Now, isn't it time you weren't here?"

By this time, it had stopped snowing and the road edges were beginning to become ever so slightly grey from the slush being flicked up by moving traffic. Fortunately, too, the main carriageways were reasonably clear, if a little slow-moving.

"Long while since you spent any real time in the old town, eh Will?" Jack said as they approached Four Lane Ends. This close to Christmas lamp-posts wore multi-coloured lights and decorations, as did trees in front gardens. That sort of thing never changed. No matter how poor people were or how difficult their lives had become, Christmas was always a time for rejoicing and celebrating. Nobody wanted others to know they couldn't really afford it.

"I suppose," William replied, paying attention to the road and looking out carefully for the turning to the school.

"You sure you know where you're heading?" Jack asked again, not overly impressed by his driving. "It would have been easier by the new motorway. What's it called? M62 or something, and that would have brought you into Normy at the bottom of Castleford Road."

"Not far from the Union, I know," William said, a little put out by Jack's insistence on efficiency, "but it's not been open very long, and I'm not so keen on motorways. Anyway, what's wrong with the old roads? They were always good enough before. We're almost there. Calder Junior and Infant School."

"You do realise that there'll be nobody here?" Jenny said, not sure why they were here at all.

"Mrs Silvester said she would be here to finish up some paperwork," William replied, "and I wanted us all to meet her."

"No car as I can see," Val observed.

"She lives close by so there wouldn't be," he said, pointing to a window by the door. "Her office is lit, so we're in luck."

"It's cold down this road," Val said, an involuntary shiver convulsing her body as her warmth met the icy blast.

"Always was, as far as I remember," Jack added. "My mate Stuart Hodgson used to live across the road on the Beckbridge estate, being in a prefab for quite some time. If you ever feel cold at home, think about living in a prefab – outside walls about two inches thick, little insulation, single glazed windows, internal walls so painfully thin you could hear a gnat fart in an adjacent room. Perishing. I remember as well, the winter of 1963, when I was in the sixth form. Some of us were allowed to have a week delivering the Christmas post, and I was sent down here. Even the regular postman didn't like it ower much. Like a rabbit warren."

"Mrs Silvester," William said deliberately as the door opened.

"William," she replied, a welcoming smile dragging them into the relative warmth. "For goodness' sake, it's Joan. Come in and shut the door. Kettle's on to give us something to warm the cockles of your heart."

With iron-grey hair and startling blue eyes, in her late fifties, she had been a head teacher at this school for fifteen or so years. Shorter than average with an ample bosom whose corsetry needed perhaps to be a little more controlling, she oozed the persona of a typical small-town junior school head teacher. She was Normanton bred and born, had trained as a teacher at Bretton Hall – Wakefield way on – and had spent the whole of her teaching life to date in this important little town. With history of the area as her passion, it could be said that she knew her stuff – industry, families, people, children, and their ancestry. At another time in another age she would have become a teacher trainer or even Her Majesty's Inspector of Schools. But, no, this is what she did, was comfortable doing, and would no doubt continue doing until she retired. Then what would she do? One step at a time.

"Cold winter on its way?" Jack said, as they settled in her office, a steaming cup of Yorkshire Tea to hand.

"I've known it colder," she replied, drinking her tea slowly. "1947 for example."

"Year after I was born," Jack said. "I remember it well."

"Remember? At one?" she queried disbelievingly.

"You'd better believe it," William laughed. "This one, I'd swear, remembers life in the womb."

"Perhaps you should come work here, then, Jack," she replied, a throaty chuckle bubbling up, "instead of your brother."

They all burst out laughing, with William not quite so sure. He never did have much of a sense of humour.

"I even like your cuppa, Mrs S," Jack added. "I can tell Yorkshire Tea anywhere."

"If ever William moves on," the head said finally as they headed for the door, "there will be a job here for you, Jack. It's always good to meet a kindred spirit."

"Smart lady," Jack observed once they were in the car heading up Castleford Road towards the churchyard. "Good talking to her."

"Can you drive past Womack's, please, William?" Val urged once they'd reached the White Swan.

"How…?" he dithered.

"Turn right," Jack advised, "and follow the road past where the Majestic Cinema used to be, past Babyland on the High Street. Then turn left on to Church Lane, where Womack's is on the corner."

"Why…?" William puzzled again.

"Flowers for the graves," they all chorused, bursting into giggles as they did.

"Do you know the way to the cemetery, Will?" Jack asked when they were en route once again. "It's—"

"Along Church Lane," William replied, "and opposite the Grammar School. I've been through it often enough."

"Ah, but," Jack insisted, "to get in – with the car?"

"Those first gates on Church Lane, opposite the school?" his brother replied, now hesitant and unsure.

"Round the corner by the school," Jenny intervened, "then left into Dalefield Avenue, and left into Neville Street. Gates are directly ahead."

"You can drive straight into the graves?" William added. "And how did you know all that?"

"Lived here longer than you, Will," she replied, a satisfied smile growing. "Visited Dad's grave often enough, and, besides, I met my husband here, eh Jack?"

"Aye," he said. "Did *that*. Just up here then Will. Mi Mam's and Granddad's graves are at the end, just…?"

A seriously puzzled look invaded his face, realising his granddad's plot wasn't as he had left it the last time he was here. He exchanged deeply concerned looks with his wife, and hurriedly left the car, followed quickly by Jenny and Val.

"My God," he muttered, his eyes filling.

"What is it, Jack?" Jenny said as she reached his side. "What's up?"

"It's mi Grandma," he said, his voice dropping to a choked whisper. "Look."

The soil in the plot had been newly turned over and covered in bunches of flowers, as if it had been turned over recently, all of which Jack had done not long before. The most significant and upsetting change had been to the headstone, with the addition of 'Marion Holmes. Beloved wife of George William Holmes. Born 1896. Died…'

This was too much for Jack. He simply stood in shocked disbelief, with tears rolling down his cheeks, the last of his close family … gone, and him not there.

-o-

"One less to visit then," William muttered.

"William!" Val hissed. "A bit insensitive to say the least. For goodness' sake, grow up."

"Just saying," he mumbled to himself.

It was funny, really, that Jack had never counted his brother as close family, not since he had grown up, anyway. Consequently, William's insensitivity over his grandma didn't register with him. Val meant more to him than his brother ever would.

They'd never had much in common, and shared neither physical family traits nor character nor personality. He supposed that were he not to see William for the *next* ten years, it wouldn't bother him too much. He shared much more with his niece and nephews than he did with *their* father, and found them a delight to be with, and certainly much livelier.

"It's only a few weeks since we saw her last," Jack said, once they had reached the sanctuary that was the Majestic Café, "and she was all right then. Why didn't someone let us know? Granddad's sister, Lizzie Hambleton, knew where we were. I don't understand."

"Out of sight out of mind, love," Jenny said when she returned from ordering at the counter. "Probably never even thought, seeing as we weren't on the scene much."

"Surely not," Val added, feeling sorry for her brother-in-law's loss.

It was like a blow between the eyes that they all felt – except for William. *He* was definitely his father's son.

"Shall you contact Lizzie?" Jenny asked.

"No point," Jack replied, gently swishing his tea round his cup. "We can't revisit it now, can we? We'll have to leave well alone. After all, she's where she wanted to be since *he* died – wi' mi granddad."

Chapter 5

"Do you ever wonder where Eric is?" Jenny asked Jack as they sat down for family lunch.

"Mi fatha?" he replied without looking up from his plate. "Why would I wonder that? I know where he is."

"No, not your Dad," Jenny replied, knowing what his answer would be. "Your half-brother – and Joyce's too for that matter."

"He lives in Normanton – somewhere – I suppose," he replied. "Why the question, and why would I want to know?"

"He'd probably be five or six years younger than you?" she continued unabashed.

"Six years and five months," he replied.

Jenny had no reason to question his accuracy. He was always right, particularly when his responses were *that* quick.

"So, you must know where he lives, then," she persisted.

"I do, as a matter of fact," he replied as he slid his cutlery into his empty plate. His plate was always clean when he had had his meal – 'clean enough not to need weshin' his granddad would always say. No waste, no mess, no arguments.

"Then … where?" she asked again, more pointedly this time.

"Mi fatha and Joyce's mother got married eventually,"

he went on, realising she wasn't going to stop pestering, "stopping their son, technically, from being a bastard, and now they live in Rothwell. Satisfied?"

"How do you know all this … stuff?" Jenny asked, a quizzical smile dancing around her mouth corners. "More to the point, *why* do you know, particularly when you reckon you don't care?"

"I mek it my business to know," he muttered, not really wanting to continue the conversation, although he would never say so in so many words.

"Don't you think you ought to try to make contact?" she suggested. "After all, he *is* your brother."

"And what would I want – or need – with another useless brother?" he replied, forcefully, ending the conversation.

Jenny knew what she was doing. A clever lass, that Jenny. She had sown a seed that her Jack would ponder upon, before he made a final decision as to whether to nurture that seed. Fifty-fifty chance, or maybe a bit less in *this* particular case.

Why had she brought this up now? What had it to do with them where he lived – or his mother and father for that matter? She was right. He was blood, but a watered-down version, and as such not acceptable. Or was it? Could he – should he – make an effort? After all, it wasn't his fault he was born to a drunken swine, any more than it was Jack's. No. He wouldn't be seeking him out. He wasn't really part of *his* family. It would take more than a splash of diluted blood to make Jack believe he could be part of his life.

"What are we doing today then, Jessipops?" Jack chuckled once the dishes had been cleared and the washing up done.

"Build a snowman, Daddy Jack," Jessie chirruped, as she closed her reading book deliberately, a huge teasing grin growing.

"Thou hussy!" he laughed. "You're teasing me, aren't you?"

"Yay!" she said, clapping her hands. "There's a bit of snow by the dustbin. Just enough to build a little snow boy."

Jack burst out into a belly-shaking guffaw that was joined by Jenny's giggle, as she drifted in to the lounge from the kitchen.

"How about," Jessie started again, tapping the side of her nose with her forefinger like she had seen Jack do on many-a-teasing time, "if we go on a visit to Oyl Park?"

"Oyl Park?" Jenny quizzed. "Where on earth is Oyl Park?"

"I suppose you called it Haw Hill Park when you were a nipper," Jack explained. "To the rest of us it was Oyl Park. A bit like t'chipoyl, I suppose, and t'coiloyl."

"Chip…?" she puzzled, a helpless shrug of the shoulders betraying her ignorance once again. "Coil…?"

"Chip hole," he explained grandly, "or to put it poshly, the shop where one obtains one's fish and chips, or scribes and farras, as my mate Tony Stathers used to call 'em when we were at college. Coiloyl is t'place where tha puts t'coil – or coal."

"You're such a mine of useless information, husband," Jenny said, a giggle underlining her mirth.

"How about Roundhay Park or Golden Acre Park, Our Jessie?" he said, picking her up with a groan and a mock show of strain. "My goodness! You are *so* heavy, I can hardly pick you up."

"Is that because you are getting old, Our Daddy Jack?" she replied, an innocent smile creasing her face.

Jack threw her into the air as usual much to her delight and with squeals of joy.

"You are strong again, Daddy," she whooped, "probably

because you eat your porridge every day, like a good boy."

-o-

"Isn't this the old tram terminus?" Jenny asked as they pulled in to the huge turn-around by Roundhay Park's rose garden and opposite the tennis courts at the bottom of North Park Avenue. "I just thought you might know, seeing as you're the fount of all knowledge and you are so much older than me."

"Cheeky mare," he laughed. "As a matter of fact, it is, but – and here's the sixty-four-thousand-dollar question for you. Even though there are posts for overhead electric wire, did trams ever turn around here?"

"Probably a trick question, my lovely," she replied with a smile, "but I would have to say that … I don't know, seeing as I probably wasn't born when they were around."

"Well," he replied, settling to his usual Encyclopaedia Britannica stance, "there you would be wrong, as trams stopped running in Leeds in 1959. The Route 3 was one of the last I believe because of the popularity of Roundhay Park, but tracks and overhead wires were never put in to this turn-around. So, really you *were* around, but not in Leeds."

"'Ark at you," Jenny teased. "Is there anything you *don't* know?"

"I came here with mi Grandma and Granddad when I was about six," he went on. "Train from Normanton and double deck tram from Leeds City Centre to Roundhay. How much more exciting could that have been?"

"I can't remember ever having been here," she admitted as she pushed Florence May through the main gates of the park in her Cindico push chair, "until I came with you, of course."

"Even *I* never came over this way much," he continued, "until I left college. No sensible transport options. In to town from Headingley, then out again to Roundhay."

"I recognise *that* pushchair," a familiar voice accosted them from behind.

"And I'd recognise *that* voice anywhere," Jack shouted back without turning around, a huge grin of pleasure setting in his face. "Is my good friend Stick with you, Our Joyce?"

"I am indeed, Jacky-boy," an equally distinctive male voice came back at him. "Fancy meeting you here."

"Very strange," Jack replied with a laugh, "given that you live only half a dozen houses down the road from us."

"So," Joyce asked, "how long is it now? Must be about the same time as us."

"Five months, give or take," Jenny replied as the double wheels on her Cindico pushchair squeaked in time with the bumpy tarmac of the main pathway towards the park's hotel. By the time they had reached the Mansion, snow had begun to fall less intermittently, and Jack's call to a cup of tea met with universal agreement. The café they were aiming for down towards Waterloo Lake would have been cheaper and more conducive to walkers with pushchairs, but the weather suggested otherwise, so the Mansion's luxury would have to do.

"Have you got your second mortgage ready, Stick?" Jack asked, a knowing smile growing.

"Second mortgage?" his friend puzzled, not understanding the reference, which did seem a little obtuse.

"Because afternoon tea here won't be cheap, my dear husband," Joyce laughed, switched on to Jack's humour.

"Be rayt," Stick replied, unusually falling in to dialect. "We're rollin' i' money since I got this job. Money for owd rope."

They all laughed at his response, drawing strange looks from the genteel folk around them, just as the waiter arrived to take their order.

"What do you think about Eric?" Jack asked Joyce, as he was half way through his second bun.

"Well," she replied, "knowing what you think of *him*, it wouldn't be your dad you're talking about. So, I deduce, my dear Watson, that you meant our half-brother."

"Well worked out, my dear Holmes," Jack said chuckling ower her smart-arsed reply. She allus was sharp, even when he sat next to her at Woodhouse Junior School. Smarter and quicker than him, he always felt, although she would have disagreed. They allus were good friends, even in the days when it didn't do for lads to have girls for friends. But then, Jack never was your ordinary sort of a lad.

"In what way?" she asked, not quite sure why he might be asking. "Thinking you might get in touch?"

"Not sure," he said, a concerned frown underlining his lack of conviction. "I just wanted to see what you thought."

"We're of a mind, Our Jack," she replied. "His parents aren't his fault. Perhaps he's a nice bloke, despite his upbringing. I'd have to think about that."

"Then let me know if you arrive at any sort of a conclusion?" Jack said, eyeing the chocolate bun Jenny had left half-eaten.

-o-

"Daddy Jack?" Jessie's little voice floated in once they had returned home to a howling blizzard of a snow storm.

"Yes, my sweet poppet?" he replied when he'd finished putting the kettle on in the kitchen. "What do you need to know?"

"I like Auntie Joyce and Uncle Stick," she said, a slight wrinkle of concern crossing her brow as she wondered whether she had got their names right. "But … who is … Eric? Is he another uncle, or is he half of a uncle?"

"Half of an uncle?" Jack answered her as he mashed the tea. "How do you mean?"

"Well," Jessie continued, "I heard Auntie Joyce say something about a poor man who was only half of a brother. Is one half *your* brother and the other half hers? Which half is yours … and couldn't you stick both halves together to share the whole one between you?"

Jack and Jennie almost collapsed trying to keep their mirth in check at the serious logic shown by their little girl.

"Well," Jack started when Jessie was nestled in his lap on the lounge settee, "you see, when my mother died…"

His voice faded away gradually and gently as the wind strengthened, eddying snowflakes in ever-tightening flurries.

"So, do I have lots of uncles now, Daddy?" Jessie's voice faded back in when Jack's explanations had been made – in four or five different ways. That's how it was with him. He needed to make sure she understood the importance of relationships in this family.

"No, my lovely," her mummy explained, "only two – your Uncle William, who is your Daddy's brother, and … Eric, who is your Daddy's half-brother. Now do you understand what half-brother means?"

"Yes Mummy," Jessie replied confidently, "like Florence May and me. She is my half-sister because we don't have the same daddy."

"Where did that one come from?" Jenny said quietly, turning to Jack as she drew her daughter to her.

"Daddy Jack is your proper daddy," Jenny went on, "because he *wanted* you, and now you are his real daughter because he loves you."

"And I love him too, Mummy," Jessie replied, disarmingly, as she rushed to throw her arms around him.

"Shall I be seeing him – both halves – soon?" she asked

after a few moments of puzzled thought.

"We don't know," Jenny explained, "because we don't really know where he lives. We'll try our best to find out, and then we'll see. All right?"

"Yes Mummy," Jessie said, as she got up and made for the hall doorway, "and now I feel like I need to read my new book. I can't let my reading stop because I have a new half-uncle."

"That's our new task then for after Christmas," Jenny said, once she'd heard Jessie's footsteps on the stairs reach their immediate destination.

"She'll forget," Jack replied, settling down with his early evening cup of tea.

"If you think that, Jack Ingles," Jenny reminded him, "then you don't know her at all. Don't forget, she learned from the master how to recall stuff at the most inopportune moments."

They both laughed quietly at the thought and made a mental note to make the search a priority after talking it through with Joyce and Stick.

Chapter 6

"Jack! Quick!" Jenny called out, a note of panic edging her words. "I think it's time. Jack!"

"Time?" he huffed as he burst through the lounge door. "As in…?"

"I think my waters just broke," she replied struggling out of her easy chair.

My word! Bang on time.

"Val?" Jack urged as the telephone receiver at his sister-in-law's house up the road burst into life. "Could you come for the kids, please? I need to take Jenny to the hospital. I have what they… Yes, it's all packed in the hallway. Five minutes? Grand."

"OK sweetie," he went on, calming his wife with his organised pragmatism. "Val will be here shortly, and then … that will be her now."

An urgent ringing of the bell drew him to the front door as Jenny pulled on her coat against the chill of a late March Saturday evening.

"Not the sort of Saturday night out I thought we might be sharing," he said, seeing her struggling with her coat, "but there'll be time later."

He knelt at her feet to help with her boots which she had leaned to accept over the last few months since Christmas.

"OK love?" Val said as she ushered the children with

their essentials out to the car. "We'll be over to see you when he's here."

Jack locked up and checked several times that the house was secure before moving round to the car.

"Jack," Jenny urged, "if you want me to have it on the lawn, take your time. Jack! Now! Please."

"Are you sure you know the way?" she asked, breathing quickly, trying hard not to let the waves of pain force her to push out the urgently protesting infant.

"How many times did I show you the route to Hyde Terrace Maternity Hospital?" he replied calmly, realising that her question was rhetorically conceived. "We won't be long. Promise."

The Outer Ring Road shot past as if it hadn't really been there, funnelling them onto King Lane and then the long roll down Stonegate Road towards Monk Bridge Road, Shaw Lane and ultimately to Headingley Lane. This area he had shuffled around frequently during his time as a student teacher, particularly the ten-pin bowling alley at the end of the Arndale Centre with its new neighbour the Kentucky Fried Chicken emporium.

Five minutes later, Hyde Park Corner and the Parkinson Building at the University were blurs on a receding memory, as they pulled into the maternity hospital's car park. As he had phoned ahead before setting off, the nursing staff was waiting at the front door, wheelchair at the ready to whisk Jenny off to her salvation, and hopefully the celebration of their newest family member's arrival.

"You can wait here Mr Ingles," a nurse advised as Jenny was spirited away. "May I get you a cup of tea?"

"No thank you," he replied as he shouldered his way into the same tiny soulless waiting room he had had to endure when Sam was born. "But will I be able to be present at the birth?"

"All things being equal," she replied, "and there being no problems, yes, but now I must be away."

The door clicked shut, to be opened almost immediately by another anxious prospective father with a little girl in tow.

"Stick! Valerie!" Jack gasped.

"Jack!" the newcomers replied as they shook hands.

"I was going to ask what you are doing here," Jack said, rolling his eyes upwards, "but I think I have a slight idea why."

"You too," his friend replied. "So, this is the cell we have to endure. Nothing like the delivery room where *this* little un came into the world. Remember?"

"How could I forget?" Jack said, a sigh bursting from his lips. "Women's toilet in the Registry Office, with our Val and the registrar in attendance. No cups of tea or last decade's magazines to shuffle through, either, eh?"

"It seems this time that everything's falling into place," Stick observed, heaving a sigh.

"Don't tempt fate, my friend," Jack warned. "You never know what's around the next corner."

"Thanks for that," Stick said, a wry smile sneaking through his optimistic bravado. "*You're* a Job's comforter and *no* mistake. Here's me thinking I've cracked it."

"Not until yon bairn's in your arms, as perfect as he can be," Jack advised, "and Joyce is in rude good health."

"He?" Stick queried. "Joyce is convinced it's going to be a boy.

"Same here," Jack agreed. "Jenny is in no doubt, and it feels … right enough, though I'm not bothered. As long as it's got two arms, two legs and one head all in the right places, I shall be all right."

"It feels like I *need* a boy," Stick said after a few minutes of calm, "to carry on the name and stuff. You know what I mean?"

"Probably, yes," Jack replied, "but it won't matter a bugger when you're dead and gone. That's what mi granddad allus used to say. They were allus convinced there was another life after this one, otherwise they wouldn't be able to see their beloved son and daughter again, like they had been promised they would."

-o-

"Mr Ingles? Mr Walker?" a nurse called, as she popped her head round the waiting room door.

Stick started, but not enough to wake his daughter who was asleep in his arms.

"Yes," Jack answered quietly for them both. "We're still here. Any news, nurse?"

"I would suggest it might be a good idea to go home," she advised, "and come back tomorrow at about three in the afternoon. It looks like it's going to be a lengthy night for them both. If anything happens in the meantime, we have your telephone numbers, and we would let you know immediately."

She turned on her heels, leaving the door ajar so she wouldn't disturb the little girl.

"Have you come in your car?" Jack asked, as he fastened his coat and made for the car park.

"Came in a taxi, so…" Stick replied, heading for the telephone.

"Oh no you don't," Jack said. "I'll take you back. The car's just over here. You can't disturb yon Valerie. So, let's get off and be ready for whatever tomorrow throws at us, eh?"

-o-

"Hello? Mr Ingles?" the telephone's voice asked at just after noon.

"Yes?" he replied, breathless from his high-speed shuffle from kitchen to hall to stop the telephone's insistent jangle.

"Mrs Ingles has delivered your baby," the voice crackled, "and they are both recovering in the ward. If you would like to visit in about an hour?"

"Thank you, yes," he gasped. "What about…?"

No time to answer as the phone clicked. Dead. No further connection. But what about the baby? Boy? Girl? He would have to wait until he got there. Got there? He needed to hurry. Shave and wash were of the essence, to make himself presentable. Keys? Where were his keys? Not in the hall. Not in the kitchen. Pockets? Bathroom?

"So, that's where you are," he quipped, sweeping them into his pocket from the en suite sink shelf.

"I wonder if Stick might want a lift?" he said to himself. "Why am I talking to myself?"

He laughed as he lifted the phone. No answer.

"We are unable to get to the phone," the answer machine crackled. "Please leave your message after…"

"Not there," Jack said quietly. "Must be at the hospital."

He unsnecked the front door, to be dragged back by the urgent ringing of the telephone.

"Just on my way, Jack," Stick assured him.

"Would you like a lift?" Jack replied quietly. "Just had the call. You too? Pick you up in two minutes? Excellent."

The run across to Hyde Terrace was different in only one way – the sense of urgency wasn't as pressing.

"No Valerie?" Jack asked as they reached the Outer Ring Road.

"Mum and Dad came over to collect her," he replied. "So, she'll be there until Joyce and Our Billy come home, although name's open for discussion."

"Brilliant," Jack cooed. "So, you got what you wanted? You can now plan your dynasty."

"I don't think so," Stick laughed. "Joyce has decided that two's just about enough."

"Jenny said that when Florence May was born," Jack smiled, "and now we have goodness knows what to add to our family. Here goes."

The afternoon was gloriously sunny but chilly, and, for a Sunday, the car park was reasonably busy. Best time to deliver, perhaps? Just one corner left to squeeze into, next to a newly-dug and manured flower bed, ready for the new season's bedding plants.

"We seem to have the main birth protagonists sitting up, and bright-eyed and bushy-tailed," Jack said as they shouldered their way into a busy ward.

"Together, in adjacent beds and cots," Stick added, a huge grin heralding his joy at seeing his wife and son.

Jenny looked tired and more than a little distressed, as Jack strode towards her and their new little son, a smile on his face but concern in his heart.

"Sweet lady," Jack said softly as he slid his arm gently around her. "Had a hard time, my beauty?"

"Yes," she said, tears welling in her eyes.

"What--?" he began to ask.

"Mr Ingles?" a deep male voice broke in. "May I have a word?"

The consultant led him out to a private room in the corridor just outside the ward doors.

"Doctor?" Jack said, puzzled as to why they should be there.

"Your wife and son have had a very difficult time, I'm afraid," he began.

"In what way?" Jack asked. "They are all right, aren't they? My wife looks very tired and upset. What's going on?"

"It was a very difficult birth," the consultant continued, trying to make light, "and your son didn't really want to join us."

"How do you mean?" Jack replied, not really under-standing. "He was stuck?"

"He was wrongly positioned in the birth canal," the consultant went on, "and so we had to use forceps to guide him gently down. They are what we call Kiellands Forceps, that give us a greater deal of control in a difficult circumstance. You will notice a very small degree of bruising around his left temple, and a slight swelling around the back of the head that we call a cephalo-haematoma."

"Are you telling me there's something wrong with my son?" Jack asked bluntly. "Will it affect his development?"

"There's nothing wrong with him," the medic said, trying to reassure him, "and when the swelling has gone, he should be fine."

"Should be?" Jack asked, unsure as to what sort of an emphasis this was. "Does that mean…?"

"Through my experience and in my opinion," he replied, putting a reassuring hand on Jack's arm, "he should be perfectly fine. Now, your wife needs you."

-o-

"Desperately tired, Jack," she said with a sigh and a wan smile.

"I know, my lovely," he replied quietly as he drew her limp body gently closer. "You've had a hard time. You've *both* been through the wringer."

"Is he all right?" she asked, more than a little apprehension dancing in her eyes. "You know … I mean…"

"Yon medic assured me that whatever damage he sustained fighting not to leave," Jack smiled, his usual humour not deserting him as he tried to lift his exhausted wife's spirits, "will be fine in a few days."

"You're not just saying that," Jenny insisted, doubt lurking in her face, "to placate me?"

"Oo 'ark at you wi' your big words," Jack said, grinning broadly. "No, my lovely, I'm not. He's got a bit of bruising to his temple because they had to use forceps to prize him out – too warm and comfortable, you see – but that will disappear in a day or two. He's asleep in his crib at the foot of your bed, so I won't disturb him – and so should you be. The nurse says you need a goodly amount of rest, so I'll leave you to it, and bring Jessie and Florence May to see you tomorrow."

"Monday?" Jenny muttered, hardly able to keep her eyes open. "What about school?"

"I've already phoned David and Irene," he replied softly. "He said not to worry, and they both send their love. I think I'd better…"

He looked over at Jenny to see she was already asleep and breathing heavily, as were Joyce and her son. Jack beckoned to Stick, who gave him the thumbs up to make their move towards the car park. They both thanked the ward sister on their way out, just catching the tail end of a heavy downpour as the carousel door spat them out on to the tarmac.

"Reminds me of the last time were in Leeds together," Stick said, a smile creasing his face.

"Great George Street?" Jack replied with a knowing nod. "Interview day? That was an amazing time, with both our futures sealed in one fell swoop."

"I don't usually like interviews," Stick said, "but I was incredibly lucky with that one."

"Like I have always said, John," Jack interrupted. "Right man, right place, right time. I knew the head in mine, so it was a lot easier for me. Yours was a *real* competition and I'm glad it turned out well for you both. After my Jenny, your Joyce is my oldest – and best – friend, and so your friendship is important to me, too."

The traffic in Headingley Lane, travelling north

towards Headingley, was busy for mid-afternoon on a Sunday, particularly around Little Sisters of the Poor church and rectory. All the broadleaf trees were again coming into full newly-painted pale green leaf, competing for attention with bursting cherry blossom buds. Soon the race would be on between the leaf husks and fallen blossom to see which would cover the grounds first, and form those annoying piles in the most inaccessible corners of the gardens.

"You off to fetch your Valerie from your Mam's?" Jack asked his friend, as they turned into their estate.

"Mi Mam and Dad have been staying with us," Stick replied. "So, hopefully mi tea will be almost ready. You?"

"I've just to nip up to our Will and Val's to scoop up my two," Jack said, "and then get their tea ready. Any idea what you're going to call your lad?"

"Open for discussion still," he said, a non-committal shrug joining them. "You?"

"Not decided," Jack replied, "but I rather fancy naming him after mi granddad, the man who made the biggest impression on me as I was growing up. Here we are. I'll drop you off and call off at Val's on the way back. Way back? That's a laugh. They only live three doors from you."

They both laughed that easy relieved laugh as they drew to a halt outside Stick's large corner plot, vowing to get together soon for a joint christening party.

"Val! Will!" Jack shouted through the letter box as he rang their door bell. "I'm back. Put t'kettle on and get some of that Yorkshire Tea on the go, please."

-o-

"Glad to be home?" Jack said, bringing tea and scones for his wife as she sat on the settee in her favourite place, nursing their new son.

"What do *you* think?" she laughed, handing over his

son to her husband, and settling back with her tea and scone.

"Well," he started, sitting down in *his* favourite seat, his son on his lap, and Jessie sitting at his feet with her favourite book on *her* lap, "obviously there is one decision we need to address though."

"Apart from what time's dinner?" she laughed.

"That's very true," he agreed, "but we need to think of a name for this young un soon, because his birth has to be registered. Any ideas?"

"No," she replied. "Not really had too much time to think about it. What about you?"

"Well," he said slowly, hoping his suggestion might be all right, "I'd like to name him after mi Granddad, George William."

He looked at her with eyebrows raised, awaiting her response.

"I like it," she said slowly. "My dad's middle name was George and my granddad was called William. So, George William works for me."

Jack sighed mentally as he smiled at the little scrap of humanity nestling, asleep, in his arms. It didn't get much better than this.

<h1 style="text-align:center;">Chapter 7</h1>

"But I don't really want him to go to nursery," Jenny insisted. "There's no need. He's only three, for goodness' sake. What's wrong with him staying here with me? He can learn more with me, and … he has lots of other children around of his age he mixes with. He has a lovely time in the back garden when Joyce brings her son, Billy, down for example. *He's* not going to nursery either. Soon enough for school when he's five."

"Just thinking about his socialising, that's all," Val said, shrugging her shoulders in her defence.

"Jack and I have decided," Jenny added, "and, anyway, it didn't hurt our Florence May. She's ready for primary school reception in September. They don't start school in some European and Scandinavian countries until age six, by the way, and it doesn't seem to harm *them*."

"How's William doing?" she went on once she had brought tea and goodies into the lounge. "Done your homework yet, Jessie."

"Just had to finish off my English composition ready for handing in tomorrow," her daughter replied. "Oh, by the way, Mummy, wasn't Daddy Jack's Uncle Jack called Holmes?"

"Yes, dear," Jenny agreed. "Why do you ask? He was killed in the second world war, in 1943."

"It's just that there's this boy in my class called Jack

Holmes," Jessie said. "Seems a bit of a coincidence, don't you think? Do you think they might be related?"

"Hello," a familiar voice boomed from the hallway, "I'm home."

By the time Jack had reached the lounge, he had a little boy in his arms and a little girl clinging to his front, her feet on his as he walked with an exaggerated gait into the room. The children were giggling uncontrollably as he tickled them until they dropped on to the hearth rug in fits of laughter.

"William's doing fine," Val said, dragging her sister back to the original question. "Tired from all this travelling, but the money's good."

"So, is *your* job permanent now, Val?" Jack asked, creeping into the conversation. "We've not heard much about it lately. In fact, we've not heard much about anything to do with your branch of the Ingles clan. Not seen a lot of you either, living such a long way away."

"Is that what you call being sarcastic, Daddy Jack?" Jessie said. "We learned about that in class yesterday, along with being ironic, but I'm not sure about the difference."

"I think you'll find not many people do," he replied, draining his mug of tea, ready to pour another. He always said he wasn't worth much until he had dispatched a couple of mugs of tea when coming in from work. "It's like when I come in from school, you find there's no Yorkshire Tea left in the caddy, only that Typhoon stuff, and you say to your mother 'That'll please Daddy Jack' when you know it won't. We do have plenty of Yorkshire Tea, don't we?"

Everyone laughed, including George William, who always did it to copy everyone else. He just had to be the same.

It was hard to keep track of a conversation that rocketed from one subject to another without wrenching the questions asked back to having answers hooked onto them. Val had become quite adept at completing questions as a matter of pride and personal satisfaction.

"It's been a long time, I know," Val said, bringing Jack back to his question about her job, "but the governors and head tell me they are close to a decision about my temporary deputy headship."

"Any indication as to which way they might jump?" Jenny asked.

"How long have you held your temporary post now, Val?" Jack said. "Only, if you are in a temporary post more than two years, your employers are legally obliged to make it permanent."

"Is that true, Jack?" Jenny asked, astonished that Val and William didn't seem to know.

"Indeed it is, my sweet pea," he replied. "If I were you, Val, I would wait until the announcement is imminent, and then speak to your area union rep."

"Do you need to speak to William about it?" Jenny urged.

"No point really," Val replied, a sigh underlining her lack of trust in his opinion and judgement. "To be honest, he's struggling with *his* job and doesn't know whether he's coming or going."

"To come back to my original question, Val," Jack asked patiently, "how long since you were given this 'temporary' job?"

"January before George William was born, I think," she replied, a rueful look nestling in her eyes.

"Three years give or take, then?" he reckoned, a resigned look, slight incline of his head and raising of his eyebrows telling his sister-in-law that they had been very lax in pressing their advantage. "In fact, forget my advice from before. I would speak to your union person as a matter of some considerable urgency. You never know."

"I'll get it," Jack said, jumping to his feet to answer a rather urgent rattle at the front door.

"My goodness me!" he was heard to say. "Who's this beautiful young lady standing on my threshold? Come in, beautiful young lady."

"Uncle Jack … purlease!" she replied with a sigh and an eyebrow lurch to the heavens.

"No kiss and a hug for an old uncle then, I take it?" he went on with a chuckle as they entered the lounge.

"I'm thirteen, for goodness' sake," she muttered, flopping into an easy chair as she dropped her school bag on to the carpet.

"Mary," Val warned her daughter, as she turned towards Jack. "I'm sorry, Jack. She's been off-hand and truculent lately. I don't know what's come over her."

"No need for apologies, dear sister-in-law," Jack said, an understanding smile creasing his face. "I think it's something we've all been through – a terminal dose of adolescence, me thinks. It'll disappear when she gets to my age. Only twenty or so years to go."

-o-

"Do you really know where?" Jenny asked Joyce on their pushchair walk to the local shops. They liked the shops at the corner of the Avenue better than the supermarket complex by the Outer Ring Road. Every shop they could need was here, on their doorstep, and over the road several miles of countryside – including a wild wooded area where a diversity of broad leaf trees abounded – stretched endlessly.

"Do you remember a while ago that I told you about my extensive network back in the old town?" Joyce reminded her. "Well, it's paid off. They've found Eric for me – for us."

"You've decided to make contact then?" Jenny puzzled,

not sure where Joyce was going with this one. "I'm still not sure whether Jack will run with it. He looks on this Eric as being the catalyst for his father leaving them, and one of the factors leading to his mam's untimely death. I'm not sure whether he would be able to forgive him for being *his* father's son."

"We said we would decide together, Jack and me," Joyce explained. "All I did was to give us the option – the choice to see or not to see. That is the question"

"But isn't it likely to force the issue?" Jenny said. "A case of option leading to need?"

"You said it yourself," Joyce replied, a wry smile spreading. "Jack won't be forced into doing something he doesn't want to do."

-o-

"Joyce found him, you know," Stick said to Jack on their way to town on the Number One Lawnswood bus from Broughton.

"Found him?" Jack replied, not understanding his reference. "I understand the *she* refers to Joyce, but who is *him*?"

"Your half-brother," his friend started to explain. "He lives in Normanton on one of the roads off Church Lane. Can't remember which one though."

"And why, Old Chap, would you think *that* snippet might be of any interest to me?" Jack said after a moment's silence. "Does this face look as if it might give a toss whether he lives in a tower or in a tree?"

"Joyce just thought that you might be interested to know," Stick replied, shrugging his shoulders and squeezing out a non-committal pursing of the lips.

He was a hard man to read, was that Jack Ingles. You never knew whether you might have him worked out, because he played his cards so close to his chest. And then, he was quite capable of telling you, eyeball to eyeball, what he thought of you and your ideas. The true feelings behind what he had to say he never let on, but then he had not changed since he was old enough to hold a spoon or an opinion.

"I understand why your Joyce has found out." Jack went on, "but I still haven't decided what I want to do yet. Perhaps we need to have a confab and arrive at some sort of a decision between us."

That had dropped a king-sized stone into his quiet little pond that, no doubt, would see rings spreading slowly. He wasn't overly keen on having his pond disturbed by happenings that weren't of his doing, but then life was full of unsolicited surprises that needed attention. Perhaps it might be a wondrously happy event discovering another brother, but what if this *chance* discovery were to lead to others? *That* possibility did not fill him with awe, although young Eric couldn't be held responsible for other brothers or sisters that might squeeze out of the woodwork.

Suck-it-up time, perhaps?

"Come on, Jacky-boy," Stick urged, breaking into a trot as they left the Queen's Hotel in their wake, urged on by the Black Prince astride his mighty steed in City Square, "our bus is dying to transport us to somewhere more conducive. Stir thi stumps."

Kerching! Kerching! That incongruously mechanical noise encouraged by a thin strip of floppy card, reassured them that soon *that* ticket would allow them to be exiting the snicket onto their estate. The thought of a couple of mugs of Yorkshire Tea and a digestive or two, followed by several sets of arms around his neck, brought a grin to his face.

"Job done," he said out of the blue, making his companion start out of his similar reverie. "Any chance of you bringing your dynasty to join ours this evening for a quick drink of summat, and a confab about where to go next?"

"To go next?" Stick asked, a mischievous smirk appearing slowly. "New job in the offing, Our Jack?"

"Smart arse," Jack laughed. "You're a man after mi own black heart, Stick Walker, and I think you know where I'm going with this."

"Half six then?" Stick offered.

"Done!" Jack said, pretending to spit on his offered hand, in time-honoured means of sealing the deal.

"It's all right," Stick laughed. "I'll take your word."

-o-

"Well that's a turn up for the books," Jack harrumphed as he opened the post one Saturday morning mid-July, not far away from the end of his academic year.

"Not *another* cheque from Littlewoods Pools?" Jenny asked, laughing ironically. "I don't know what we'd do with all that extra cash."

"A demand rather than an offer, I'm afraid," he replied slowly. "Our solicitor has received what he calls a 'request' for maintenance from my ex-wife. Not an unreasonable amount, as it turns out, although any request is unreasonable in my view."

He passed over the correspondence as he sat back with a cup of coffee, unusually, waiting for her opinion.

"What will you do, Our Jack?" Jenny said as she skipped through the letter.

"Pay it, of course," he replied. "After all, he is my son. I can't see him wanting even though finding a job doesn't seem to agree with her."

"What must he be now? Sevenish?" she replied, realising what a wonderful life he would have had if he'd been theirs. She didn't begrudge the hundred pounds he would pay, but it would have been better spent on *their* children. Would she *have* to find work finally to help pay their extra bills? She knew she would one day, but would she want to now she was settled in her lovely routine?

Their friend Joyce thought she might go back to work at some stage, but Jenny had never had to work before, and she worried how she might take to it – whether she might take to it at all. Jack had always reassured her that he would support her if she decided to find work, but it would have to be her decision.

"Will you want me to go out to work to help pay for this extra money we'll have to find?" she asked him, probably knowing the answer already.

"I'm thinking of sending you out to work," he replied, deadpan, "and me staying at home to cook and bake."

They both laughed.

"We'd be dead in a few days," she said, eyes looking to the heavens. "Particularly you. Seriously, though?"

"Who'd look after our children, particularly George William?" he answered, his serious face taking over. "Yours is the most important job in the world. You would have to fulfil two conditions, really. George William would need to be at school full-time, and, more importantly, you would really have to *want* to. Whatever you choose to do, I want you to be happy."

"But what about…?" she began.

"The money?" he interrupted, a smile signalling his happiness. "We can afford it so you don't *need* to go out to work, my sweet. Enough said about that. The next very important issue that needs attention is --"

"What time's lunch?" *she* interrupted, knowing full well what was coming next.

"How come you can read my mind so easily?" he asked.

"Two things, my man," she replied, touching the side of her nose with her forefinger. "I'm a woman, and women know everything their men are thinking, and I'm intuitive.

No contest."

"I love you, Jenny Ingles," he laughed.

"So you should," she laughed back, leaping on him unexpectedly, threatening to tickle him to death.

-o-

"I've heard, Fatha, as folks are asking questions abaht me," the young man said. "'As thy any knowledge as to why?"

"Abaht thee?" Eric, his father, answered "Why does thy ask me? What would I know abaht what thy gets up to? Don't thee forget, lad, that it wor thee as decided tha wanted to live on thi own, wiyout thi mother an' me. Thy choice. Thy 'as to live wi' it."

"T'lad's onny askin' thee a civil question, 'usband," the lad's mother pointed out. "Tha's allus said 'e should come to thee fust ifn ever anything wor botherin' 'im. Now's thi chance to show 'ow much on a fatha thy is."

"All rayt. All rayt," the lad's father said. "I'll set mi mind to it and ask around. All rayt? Now, can a man ayt 'is tea in peace?"

"'Ave you any notion, Mam?" the lad asked as they went into the front room, away from his father's company. It had become more and more difficult for him to talk to his father over recent months, ever since he decided he wanted a place of his own. Not too much to ask at going on twenty-five, was it? He had a good job at Sharlston pit as a trainee engineer, hoping to go on to Whitwood Tech to get his qualifications – that piece of paper that would take him out of the mines altogether. She was so proud of her son's ambition that she wished his father shared. Too proud to admit, no doubt, that his son was doing something that *he* should have done many years before. And what was he doing now? Same job as he had done for the last thirty years or so.

He often sat and pondered ower what his other sons

might be doing now, and where they lived. Grandchildren? Did he have grandchildren? He would probably never know. Still, not one to dwell.

"The onny thing I can think on is thy half-sister and brother," the lad's mother replied.

"Half…?" the lad said, almost under his breath, not understanding what she was trying to say. "Is there summat tha wants to tell me, Mother?"

Chapter 8

"**D**addy Jack?" Jessie asked in that wheedling drawled sort of a way that she told him she needed something from him.

"Yes, my soon-to-be-eleven-year-old sweet pea," he replied, a smile curling his lips. "What do you need, and how big a loan do I need to take out to pay for it?"

"I think I'm going to get into trouble in school," she replied quietly, ignoring his attempt at humour.

"Why?" he asked, sitting up to take notice. "What are you about to do wrong, Jessie? You've never been in trouble before – ever. So, what…?"

"There's this girl in school," Jessie started, "who keeps on picking on me, and won't leave me alone."

"Have you told your teachers?" he asked, perturbed to hear what she had to say.

"They never listen," she explained. "They always say there *is* no bullying in the school, and that we have to learn to get on together."

"I'll come in to school and have a word," Jack said, leaping to his daughter's defence.

"It won't work, Daddy Jack," she interrupted, wise beyond her years. "They'll say I'm making it up and that there is no bullying. Same thing happened to two of my friends a few weeks ago."

"But," he protested, "I can't have my daughter treated

like this.”

"It's all right,” she assured. “I'll handle it in my own way, in my own time. I just wanted to warn you in case there is any 'fallout'."

Fall out? What did she mean? How could *his* little daughter who had been brought up to respect everybody's right to peace and happiness without interference, be having to deal with this sort of stuff on her own? However, Jack had always had to deal with whatever was thrown at him without *his* parents' involvement, so…

"Keep me posted, please, Jessie?” he asked, wanting to protect her from the worst of other people's excesses.

"You must promise me not to interfere if I do,” she warned. "Promise? Really promise?”

"Of course,” he agreed reluctantly, “but if I see any signs of your not sorting stuff out, I *will* step in. Agreed? Really agreed?”

"Agreed,” she replied, “but only if you don't tell mum.”

-o-

"What is it with schools and teachers these days, eh Stick?” Jack asked his friend as they boarded the Number One Broughton bus in City Square.

"How do you mean, Jack?” he replied, not understanding his reference, as serving teachers.

Jack explained his daughter's situation after swearing him to secrecy.

"It's not just a case of nowadays, as you well know, Jack,” Stick said once they had taken their seats. “I was picked on in the top class of junior school because some idiot thought it was a hoot to make fun of my name. It continued into the Grammar School, until *I* sorted it out, because I knew the teachers would do nowt about it.”

"How did you get them to stop?” Jack asked, intrigued to know.

"A punch in the mouth tended to do the trick," Stick explained, a deadpan face belying his words, "It's surprising how effective not being able to talk can be."

Jack burst out laughing, silencing the bus and urging its passengers to turn around to seek out the only person so happy at this time on a dour work morning.

"You see," Jack said, "*that* makes me concerned what she means by 'handle it in her own way'. Still, I've no doubt she *will* sort it out. Her old man always used to. Mi granddad always used to say that there were two ways to handle bullies. The first was to ignore them, and, eventually they'd give up. If they didn't give up, *then* a smack in the gob would usually get them to take note."

"A wise man your granddad," Stick laughed as he prepared to disembark. "Enough of this frivolity. Later?"

"Fraid not," Jack replied with a grimace. "Rugby training wi' t'little uns after school."

"Rugby? At this time of year?" Stick replied with a gasp. "Shouldn't it be running or cricket or summat else seasonal?"

"Preparation for next year, old chap," Jack said almost seriously. "Got to win the Webster Shield this coming year. David, my boss, says so. See you later."

The Number One shrugged off its passengers and chugged away to the tune of its cracked still reverberating bell, as Stick Walker trudged across Town Street to Old Lane and his school. The sun was beginning to warn the good citizens of Leeds that they were about to experience one of the warmest days they had had for many a year.

-o-

"Can I have a word, Jack?" David said as he shouldered his way in to the empty staff room. "Something important's come up that will affect us both significantly."

"Sounds ominous," Jack replied with a grimace. "So,

we won't be getting a large salary increase anytime soon, then?"

"I received word from Great George Street that, at the beginning of next academic year," David continued, ignoring Jack's usual flippant response, "Mr Barchester will retake his post as head of this school."

"So, we've effectively been given twelve months' notice," Jack said. "That means that you will be moving on and I will have two choices."

"This is one of the things I will miss about you, old chap," David said with a rueful smile. "You can always be relied upon to hit bull's eye with your first shot."

"Have they anywhere in mind for you, Boss?" Jack smiled, always pragmatic and practical.

"John Holt at Cross Flatts Junior is retiring next summer," David replied, "and I am to take over. Bigger school, but…"

"There's already a deputy in post?" Jack interrupted.

"You got it," his friend said, shrugging his ample shoulders.

"Does this signal the end of a beautiful friendship, then?" Jack asked, knowing what the answer would be.

"Of course not, daft bugger," David said. "We've been through too much together, and, besides, we're family. Can't get rid of family, no matter what."

"And me?" Jack said, dropping quickly back to earth. "Do I take it there's nothing lined up for me?"

"You've two choices, I'm afraid," David said with a shrug and a grimace. "Tried to get us a billet together, but there aren't any going, unless you are willing to take a pay cut."

"Can't do that. Old boy," Jack replied. "My wife is now living up to my salary, and that's how I like it. I'm not sure whether I want to work as Mr Barchester's deputy either. Don't get swelled-headed when I say it's been brilliant working with you. More of a team, a partnership, than it would be with Mr Barchester."

"Whatever happens," David assured him, "you won't lose out. I'll see to that."

"But you've no idea how yet," Jack said quietly. "That I understand, but it may come down to looking elsewhere within this authority – or without."

"Bit of advice from someone who's a lot older and much wiser and more experienced?" David offered with a laugh.

"Who had you in mind, mon capitaine?" Jack replied, a guffaw about to erupt. "Me?"

They sat back, tea in hand, relaxed in each other's company. This would be a hard act to follow. Their two families hadn't been in each other's company for some time, so Jack thought it was about time he organised one of his famous get-togethers.

"That sounds like a wonderful idea," David agreed. "Imogen Rose and Florence May have celebrated their joint birthday only once, but that's March and this is summer. *That* we should do next birthday. After all, they will be six."

"As for now," Jack suggested, "second week of the summer holiday? How would you fancy a few days at the White Lodge in Filey?"

"Capital idea," David agreed. "Will you book, or shall I?"

-o-

"Upheaval again in the not-too-distant future, I'm afraid, my sweet," Jack said once he was home and settled in his castle, drawbridge raised and boarders repelled. Their garden was still a riot of colour, with the little waterfall tinkling away in the background, as he sat shorted and tee shirted under their multi-coloured parasol, his bare toes wriggling in the late Saturday afternoon sunshine

"And what does that mean?" she asked, not really expecting anything untoward. "You said we were all right. Is it to do with money, my man? Are we short?"

"Nothing of the sort, lovely," he replied, putting his arm about her and pulling her close as he explained what David had told him.

"So, he's coming back then?" Jenny said, disappointed at the news, for Jack's sake. "His mother must have died. Top and bottom, Jack – do we have to find somewhere cheaper to live?"

"We don't have to find *anywhere* else to live," he reassured her, explaining the two options that affected *him* only. "So, you see, I *could* stay with Mr Barchester – but what I have to ask myself is do I *want* to stay with him?"

"Would there be anything wrong with being his deputy?" Jenny asked, not sure where the problem lay. "He doesn't smell, does he?"

"No, he doesn't," Jack replied quietly, "but he doesn't listen or allow initiative either. Dichotomy, really."

"Di…?" Jenny asked, a puzzled frown descending."

"Problem of which way to jump," he explained, shrugging his shoulders, undecided what his next move might be. "It might be as well just to sit tight and suck it and see. We can't lose anything by doing that – except … time."

"Then what?" she asked again. "Start applying for other jobs *again*? Why is nothing ever simple?"

"At head teacher level," he replied, "everything is quite straight forward, because heads are somewhat indispensable. For everybody else, you are lucky if you *have* a job. I can remember one of my head teachers once saying to me 'Jack, I know you could do my job but I'm damned sure I couldn't do yours'. Not the same any more. We'll have to wait and see when the time comes.

"Can anyone tell me if I have any children?" he said, a laugh ready to tease its way out of his body. "I don't seem to have seen any of them for months."

"Jessie's got piano practice until half four," she began to reel off their interests other than school and family. "Florence May is having tea with Grandma Flo and Grandpa Jim and will be staying over until tomorrow, and George William, bless his cotton socks, is in his bedroom playing with his toys. So, if you would like to be savaged by a little boy who can't get enough of his daddy, that's where you should start."

"Georgie boy," Jack yelled as he bounded upstairs. "Where's my little man?"

"Daddy!" a little screech echoed instantly. "You're here!"

Jenny smiled. How that lovely man adored his children.

-o-

"And don't you ever see your mother, Our Joyce?" Jack asked over dinner at their friends' house. "I mean … ever?"

"She had a choice to make, Jack," she replied, her brow furrowing to show how serious the subject had become, "and she made the wrong one when she abandoned us to live with … well, you know. Your feelings about your father are well-documented."

"If you're thinking about seeking out your brother," Stick said, not sure about their hesitation, "then, does it *have* to involve his – and your- mother, Joyce?"

"No," Jack replied in that slow, drawled way he had of trying not to be condescending, "because –"

"He doesn't live with them," Jenny chipped in. "Does he?"

"Spot on, Our Jen," Joyce added. "We don't have to see either of our parents, Jack. Which leads me to wonder why the shiniest apple in their fruit bowl lives on his own?"

"Does this perhaps tell us that he left of his own free will," Jenny added, "and he is not perhaps as bad as we at first thought?"

"I already know his address," Jack pointed out, matter-of-fact as usual, as if it had been a foregone conclusion all along, "and if we are going to do it, I think we should write him a letter. Sooner rather than later."

"A phone call maybe?" Joyce added. "Quick and easy."

"I think a letter would be better," Jack repeated. "Just think. What would *you* prefer? A phone call from a stranger whom you don't know, putting you on the spot, or a letter that you might deal with at your leisure?"

"Point taken," she replied, recognising the sense in his reasoning. "Will you do the honours, then?"

"Is the Pope Roman Catholic?" Jenny said, giggling at the idea of *not* asking him to do what he was best at. "He's probably got it done in his head already."

Jack simply smiled.

-o-

"Oo the bloody 'ell do they think they *are*?" half-brother Eric boomed as he read the contents of Jack's letter. "Why the bloody 'ell would I want to jump just because they've written a letter. 'Ave we just won t'pools that they want to see me now? Bugger off! I've just got rid o' one lot o' folks wantin' to control mi life. So I'm sure as 'ell not tekin' on another lot."

"Didn't you stop to think that they might have onny just found out that you don't live with your parents any more?" his lady friend argued. "That they might genuinely want to meet *you*, their brother? Don't forget that they are your brother and sister from both sides of the family, without being brother and sister themselves? That's got to mean something, hasn't it? At least, it must be reasonably unusual. Worth a go, don't you think?"

Eric sat reasonably quietly and thought for a while, muttering and mumbling as he stretched out in his favourite chair by the hearth, watching the flames switching on the tiny globes of soot hanging on tenuously as the yellow tongues of flame licked the fire back in passing.

"I can't reply any road," he muttered, "because t'pieces of yon letter are in t'back o' t'fire."

"I can remember t'address," Ellen replied. "I knew you'd sound off, and then, once you'd thought a bit on it, you'd perhaps come round to see sense. They've even made it easier by putting a phone number."

"Smart arse," he harrumphed. "Why are there so many smart arses in the world who seem to think they know best?"

"Probably because we do," she replied, a self-satisfied smile spreading. "Well?"

"Well what?" he said, lifting his face towards her.

"Are you going to pick up that telephone," she insisted, "or am I?"

"I'll do it missen, in mi own good time," he replied.

"Aye," she sneered, "and we all know when *that's* going to be."

"For goodness' sake, woman," he said. "Where's t'bloody phone?"

–o–

"Well," Jack said, scratching his head as he replaced the telephone receiver, "that's a turn up and no mistake."

Chapter 9

"Where did you get the idea of coming here for your summer holiday, Jack?" Joyce asked. "I would never have thought of a place like this."

"Been here once or twice before," Jack replied as he luxuriated in the early afternoon sun, drinking his favourite Yorkshire Tea. "Once with David and Irene and their bunch. The White Lodge in Filey's always held a fascination for me."

"I'm glad you asked us to come," Stick said. "The kids love it, especially the castle you've helped them to build."

"Double Jessie are getting on well," David added. "So, no need for us to amuse there."

"I don't think they'd take too kindly to us interfering with their grown-up talk," Jack said, a laugh beginning to bubble. "After all, they are ten going on twenty-eight."

"Mammy," Jessie said urgently to Jenny, "will you please stop our George from picking his nose and threatening to wipe it on us? It's disgusting, and we don't like it, do we Jessie?"

"Mammy! Mammy!" George William complained in tears.

"*Now* what's the matter?" Jenny asked, unable to attend to her cup of Yorkshire Tea.

"My arm hurts," he whimpered. "Jessie pushed me, and I felled in a nole."

Jenny turned sharply, concern etched on her face, fearing the worst. Her son stood in front of her, tears welling in his eyes as his unmoving right arm hung limply by his side.

"Oh no!" Jenny groaned, fearing their holiday would be swamped by a hospital visit.

Jack took over in an instant, dropping to his knees to inspect his son's suspected injury.

"Let me see," he insisted quietly. Seeing his child injured brought back memories of Mary's 'nole tripping' on their visit a year or two before. Resisting the urge to make light of his poorly elbow, which he believed *wasn't* broken, he felt gingerly around the small lump that had arisen. His son, distracted by David's face-pulling, didn't react to Jack's insistent prodding, but his face did light up when Stick and Joyce turned up with a handful of 99s – chocolate flake and all – to hand out to the children. Not one to miss out, George William strangely forgot about his 'injury', and, grasping the offered ice cream cone in his right hand, he began to wrap his lips and tongue around its delectably soft white exterior.

"Panacea for all ills," Joyce said, a hugely satisfied grin splitting her face. "Better than *all* the pain killers in *all* the medicine shops in *all* the world. Wonderful."

"And can I assume," Jack asked, a doubting bubble enclosing his head, "that *all* adults are banned from consuming *all* ice cream cones?"

"No, they're not, Old Boy," David piped up, holding up a matching number of cones, tubs and choc ices in a dainty brown paper carrier bag. "Would I have you miss out on these delights?"

"Would you stop calling me 'wood eye'?" he laughed, rapidly unwrapping his favourite choc ice as they all burst out laughing when the eager adults began *their* demolition of those wonderful ice creams.

The adults lounged in their comfy deck chairs on the edge of this glorious beach, watching their youngsters digging furiously to finish their sandcastle before the tide overcame its battlements. All this time, the two Jessies chatted away about things important to them, nibbling the remnants of their 99s as they sucked the remains of the ice cream through the pointy ends of their cones, oblivious to all else around them.

"Have you ever considered one of them new-fangled package holidays to southern Spain?" Stick asked Jack as he sipped his hot coffee and nibbled his Tunnock's caramel wafer biscuit.

"No fear!" Jack shot back quickly. "If I could catch a Number 7 bus from outside mi front door, maybe Spain might be an option, but mi Uncle Jack was killed in an aeroplane in t'war, and I've not trusted them ever since. Besides, I've heard it's hot there in the summer. Can't do with all that heat and sun and … foreign food."

"That's over thirty years ago, old chap," David laughed, prompting Jack to shrug and smile. "I have it on good authority that the machines these days have improved somewhat since the war. It can be cheaper than going to … Filey, and it would be unusual to be chased by a German Messerschmitt fighter plane."

They all burst out laughing at what David had said and at the face Jack pulled in response.

"I still like Filey," he emphasised, to the 'hear hears' from everyone else.

-o-

"Fantastic holiday, with my most favourite person on earth," Jack sighed as they headed for home almost in convoy from Filey.

"Stick will be pleased and proud," Jenny laughed.

"Daft beggar," he replied, trying hard not to laugh in

return. "What about you, Jessie and Florence May and George William? Did you have a good time?"

"Yay!" the two younger ones shouted.

"Been joyed it," George agreed. "Like sand and diggin'."

"You've not answered, Jessie," her mother picked up straight away. "Haven't you had a good time?"

"Mmm," she replied half-heartedly after a moment or two's hesitation. "It was all right … I suppose."

She had descended recently into early adolescence and had become more than somewhat awkward in most things. Jack didn't like what he was hearing and was on the point of giving her a telling-off. Jenny recognised his attitude at once but stopped him with a look before he had had time to cause a rift.

"We'll be going on holiday again real soon," she flashed at her daughter, "so if you'd prefer to spend time with your biological father while we're away enjoying ourselves in the sun, tell me now and I'll arrange for you to spend the fortnight with *him* while we are away getting brown and lazing on the sands and splashing in the sea in Southern Spain."

"What's the matter, Jessica?" Jack cut in sharply, seeing as his daughter wasn't about to answer any time soon. "Cat got your tongue?"

Jenny's steadying hand on his thigh reminded him not to be so hard on her, particularly as she caught the glisten of tears beginning to well in her eye corners. The other two had fallen silent, realising their sister was in trouble. They enjoyed the banter and rough and tumble of family life, but they were still as one where conflict was concerned.

"We'll soon be home Jessiepops," Jack assured her, his voice quieter and more conciliatory. "Then you'll be in your own room and…"

"I should like to be able to spend more time with Jessie," she said quite simply, "because I don't have any friends at school, and I can just … talk with her."

Jenny threw a surprised glance at her husband to tell him that this was news to her.

"But I thought…" Jenny said, gobsmacked at this unexpected revelation. She felt sure she was happy at school and had a good many friends.

"No, Mummy," Jessie replied cautiously slowly, "that's what you *wanted* to think. I never said that I even *liked* the place. Is there any chance I might go to Jessie's school, even if it's only until the end of top class?"

"Not a problem getting in," Jack warned her, "but how would you get there and back?"

"Couldn't you take me … in the car?" she offered after a moment's thought, a soft, almost pleading tone to her voice.

"I suppose I…" Jenny started to answer.

"Bit difficult really, Jess," Jack replied, interrupting his wife quickly. "Mum's got the car, as you know, to take to and bring back from school. You could come on the bus with me?"

"Anything, Daddy Jack, anything," she replied tearfully.

Now he *knew* she was serious. She had never used emotions as either tool or weapon in her dealings with other people, and her unhappiness cut him deeply. She was his daughter in all but birth, so he had to do whatever was necessary to restore her happiness and her *faith* in him as her 'fixer'.

"I tell you what," he said after much deliberation, "I'll have a word with Jessie's dad, who happens to be family, as you know. I feel sure we'll be able to work something out."

"Thank you, Daddy Jack," she said, her smile returning slowly. "I knew I could rely on you."

Jack and Jenny exchanged knowing glances. They just *had* to sort out their little girl's problem, no matter what. How remiss had they been not knowing?

"That's extraordinary," Jack gasped, as he spoke to David on the phone, once t'children had been packed off to bed. "So, your Jessie feels exactly the same way as ours? This is me being cynical, but do you think there's any chance of … collusion between…?"

"No, I don't think so," David replied, sure that he could trust his daughter's truth at least. "She's not one to become upset easily about something so fundamental. Would your lot like to come over to meet and spend the day with my lot, and we'll try to find a way around it?"

"Sounds like a plan," Jack agreed with a laugh. "How's about we bring the sort of take-away that everybody likes, then Irene doesn't have to spend endless hours catering?"

"Irene says that that's a good idea," David said, "and that you are a wonderfully thoughtful man, though I think she's had too much to drink."

Jack laughed as he replaced the receiver, explaining his conversation to Jenny.

"You're going to miss him when you're no longer working together," Jenny said, a deep sigh signalling her concern.

"Be rayt," Jack replied in his usual matter-of-fact way. There were upsetting yet exciting times ahead that he would accept but turn to his advantage no doubt. He had had to learn a hard lesson about loyalty, had Our Jack – one that would rankle but would make him a better colleague and friend. Times in education generally had changed radically over the last few years and most of it not for the better.

Too many times non-educational politicians had stuck their collective oar into a process that they tried to control but had no idea what they were doing. Consequently, services and organic developments had suffered, with rapid deterioration the result. Oh, for folks who knew what they were doing!

"If this business follows its logical course," Jenny went on, "I'd be more than happy for you to take the car so that Jessie could come with you to school and…"

"And what about our Florence May," Jack asked, "and your Val's three?"

"Jessie's welfare and happiness come first," she insisted seriously. "Besides, I can walk with Flo and Our George. Val's three are now two as Joey is old enough to look after himself, and Ed can walk to school or bus it. Mary, I should imagine, would be more than happy to take herself off to school with her mates."

"Let's just wait until we've spoken to David this weekend," Jack said quietly, "and then we can decide. Agreed?"

"I'm still not overly enamoured with leaving the car parked at school all day," he went on after a bit of thought, "when *you* could be using it."

-o-

"And it came as more than a bit of a shock to find out *our* Jessie had felt the same about school as *your* Jessie," Irene said, just about controlling her emotions. "We were always convinced she loved it and had lots of friends."

"This Chinese is excellent," David mumbled through a mouthful of egg fried rice and sweet and sour.

"There seemed to be a good deal of relief when they saw each other," Jenny added with a slight smile. "Thank goodness they have each other."

"We don't have take-aways that often," Jack replied, "but this one hits the spot every time – and the chips are to die for. I can't believe they're twice-fried."

"What do you think we ought to do about it?" Irene asked, genuinely at a loss as to which way to go.

"I think we'll try these again," David said, finishing off

his last two pieces of sweet and sour chicken. "The sauce is excellent."

"I'm genuinely not sure," Jenny added. "It's got me puzzled."

"I think next time there needs to be more egg-fried rice," Jack said, licking his lips as he slid his cutlery into his clean plate, fork before knife. "No need to wesh up, as mi Granddad Jud used to say. Plate's clean."

"Have you two heard anything we've said," Irene said, turning on their husbands, "or have you been more concerned with filling your bellies?"

"Of course we have my lovely," David replied. Licking the last vestiges of sauce from his mouth. "You were talking about … booking the next jaunt to … Filey?"

"Nay, be fair. You can't begrudge us our tea," Jack said, leaping in to support his pal. "We've not eaten for at least … two hours."

Sighing deeply in unison, Irene and Jenny cast their glances in supplication to the heavens as their husbands chuckled in glee.

"Anyway, Jacky-boy and I have sorted it out," David replied as he shuffled back comfortably into his armchair, hands together supporting his full belly.

"Sorted it out?" Irene scoffed sarcastically. "When? During tea?"

"Nope," Jack piled in. "It so happened that yesterday, I had a phone call from Jim Arkwright telling me they were to get a brand spanking new … Rover, and would I like to take the 95 off his hands?"

"And when was this?" Jenny said, a disbelieving frown crossing her brow.

"You remember yesterday?" he smiled. "When you were in the back garden inspecting the insides of your eyelids in that poofily comfortable reclining chair?"

"Yes?" she replied guardedly. "What of it? I was

resting."

"Well, that's when he phoned," Jack said, sitting back on his self-satisfied smile. "They take delivery in two weeks, and as he would get next to nothing for his old car, he would prefer to gift it to us rather than – his words – line some leech's pockets at *his* expense. We can collect it on the same day. Better then because they've only one garage, and he's always garaged his cars."

"This means then that…?" Jenny said, sitting bolt upright.

"We will have *two* cars," he replied, an enormous smile splitting his face, "and I can take Jessie to school with me."

"In the meantime," David jumped in quickly, "I have had a word with Harry Butcher, our Jessie's head teacher, who's a long-time friend of mine, and he said they would be very pleased to take *your* Jessie as they have space in the top class from September – same class as *our* Jessie. Cool, eh?"

"I don't know what to say, really," Jenny added quietly, unable to grasp what she had just heard.

"Perhaps you might start with what a clever husband and a brilliant cousin-in-law you have," Jack offered, "to have wiped away an enormous obstacle to our daughter's future happiness with such brilliant…"

"Don't push your luck, buster," Jenny replied as they all burst out laughing.

"Why is everyone laughing, Daddy Jack?" Jessie asked as she entered the lounge, closely followed by her friend … Jessie.

"OK my little poppet," Jack started. "Come and sit over here and I'll explain."

-o-

"And you've done all that for me, Daddy Jack?" Jessie said once her tears had been wiped away and a happy glow had returned to her face.

"Can't think of anyone else in the world I'd rather do it for," he replied. "After all, you *are* my daughter, and besides, most of the work has been done by your Uncle David. He deserves most of the credit."

"But…" she stammered, confusion beginning to reassert itself, "is Jessie's school a nice one? I mean, will I be able to like it again, and perhaps make … friends?"

"That's up to you, my lovely," Jenny replied. "It's not something you have given to you as a … present. You've got to work at it, too, you know. But then, I'm sure you will."

"When do I start?" Jessie asked eagerly.

"New term in September," Jack said, pleased with the outcome and with the effort put in by his good friends. They had *always* shown their worth. "Day one in September, you will be riding with me in Grandpa Jim's old car to your new school, after picking up Jessie Two en route, and then…"

Chapter 10

"But Dad," Joey insisted, "I'll soon be twenty-years-old. How can that be too young to learn to drive?"

"It's too young because you haven't any money to pay for driving lessons," William replied. "That's how."

"But," Joey continued, "isn't that where *you* come in?"

"And how do you reckon that one, for goodness' sake?" William harrumphed through an irritated scowl.

"*You* could teach me," Joey said, with what he thought would be a winning smile, enough even to melt the hardest heart.

Unfortunately, with his dad it didn't work quite that way, because with him nothing was ever straight forward or easy.

"I've neither the time nor the energy nor the money," William replied as he fobbed his first-born off with excuses.

"Nor could you care less either," Joey muttered as he sidled out of the front door, expecting the inevitable.

"I bet Uncle Jack would teach me," he added as he strode down the drive towards his aunt's place. Why did it always have to be a struggle to get his father to agree to *anything*? His uncle understood him so much better.

"Now then Joseph," Jack greeted his nephew as he ushered him into the lounge. "Long time no see. Coffee?"

"Yes please, Uncle Jack," he replied, eyes lighting up.

"Milk and four sugars please."

"Four…?" Jack gasped. "Turning into a sugar monster are we?"

They both laughed, easy in each other's company.

"Mind you," Jack went on. "I can sympathise wi' that. Can't stand the taste o' the stuff missen, either."

"Uncle Jack," Joey started solemnly, "I…"

"Have a proposition for you my boy," Jack interrupted. "Don't you think that, at soon-to-be-twenty, it's about time you learned … how to drive? Only, you're getting on a bit now, and the older you get, the harder it is to learn to become a *good* driver. Look at your Dad for example."

Joey let out a huge guffaw at the image conjured in his head. Why was it that his Uncle Jack always knew the right things to say, and could always make him laugh, even when there was nothing worth laughing about?

"So," Jack went on, "I thought *I* would teach you. If you're up for it, that is?"

"Up for it?" Joey enthused. "It was only this morning I … You've been talking to Mum, haven't you?"

"Well," his uncle replied, a smile beginning to poke its face around his mouth, "I might have heard a little bird. I'm guessing your Dad's not in favour, then?"

"He won't either pay or teach," Joey replied, his shoulders slumping as his voice dropped. "Sometimes I wonder if he cares at all."

"Oh, he cares all right," Jack went on. "It's just that he doesn't know how to show it, and he is quite worried that you're growing into your own man, and very soon will not need *his* input at all."

"Then, why…?" the lad said, puzzled.

"Don't forget, Joey," Jack began to explain, "that I had a truly uncaring father all my life, so I know how it feels. Enough of that. Do you want to become a good driver or not?"

"Too bloomin' right I do!" Joey gushed.

"Then this is what we must do…" Jack started, his voice trailing off into quiet explanation. Conspirators together.

-o-

"Rover 95!" Joey said, hissing his adulation for both uncle and car. "If you'd asked me which car I should like to own, it's standing right before me, and in the right colour – British Racing Green. Wow!"

"Don't tell anyone else yet," Jack whispered, looking back over each shoulder in turn as if to check no-one was listening. "Promise?"

"But, you haven't *told* me anything yet, Uncle Jack," the lad replied, chuckling as he did so.

"Promise?" Jack insisted, even more quietly.

"I promise," Joey agreed solemnly. "But why?"

"If you pass your test first time – and I will be the judge of when you are ready to take the test -," Jack explained, a serious look descending, "at the end of the next academic year, this lovely Rover 95 will … be … yours."

Joey's mouth dropped open in shock, finding it very hard to speak.

"Wha…?" he uttered finally, the shock just allowing him to breathe.

"By then I will have no need of it, because Jessie will be leaving primary to take that hallowed path to greater things," he replied. "Then I can go back to my glorious bus travel again."

"I don't know what to say, Uncle Jack," Joey gasped. "That's uncommonly generous of you."

"You'll be doing me a favour, really," Jack said. "We don't need two cars, and I can do without the financial burden of running two. So, is it a deal? Your silence for a Rover 95?"

"My god, yes," Joey hissed, looking over his shoulder, to Jack's peals of laughter.

"I'll make sure the tank's filled with juice before you take it on, and that it's taxed for the year," Jack went on. "You'll have to be responsible for the insurance. I'd ask your dad once again, when the time is right."

Eye brows raised conspiratorially, and head cocked to one side, he put his arm around Joey's shoulders and nodded sagely.

"Stick with me, Kid, and you'll be OK," Jack continued in his usual pathetic attempt to look and sound like Humphry Bogart.

Joey burst into fits of laughter at his uncle's caricature of the screen icon, and decided it was time for another cup of coffee and one of his uncle's favourite chocolate digestive biscuits.

"I don't have fun like this with my Dad," Joey said as he supped and nibbled. "There are times when I could be forgiven for thinking he doesn't care much at all."

"Fortunately, I suppose, it wouldn't do for us all to be the same," Jack replied, taken by his nephew's concern. "He doesn't see the world in the same way as I do, and so doesn't see that you need to have lumps of ... fun, every day."

"You don't even *look* like your brother," Joey said, his whispered reply betraying his sadness.

"My response could have been 'Thank Goodness', I suppose," Jack laughed. "To be serious though, he *does* care, but he hasn't yet worked out that he needs to show it on a daily basis. If you would like a bit of nonsense at any time, you could of course drop down here. Door's always open."

"Thanks for all of this, Uncle Jack," Joey said as he made for the door. "I feel a lot better now."

"It's the Yorkshire Tea and digestive as does it," Jack

said with a laugh. "I warned you it would start to get you one day. It doesn't matter that you had coffee, because you've spent time in the temple to its delights."

Joey chuckled as he ambled down the drive, a happier smile stealing across his face. He was a caution was his uncle and no mistake. Why couldn't there be more Uncle Jacks in the world? Why wasn't *his* father more like him?

-o-

"What do you think you're playing at, Jack?" his brother's voice hissed into the telephone receiver.

"Actually, William," Jack replied lightly, "I'm trying to hold this phone and not allow my dunked digestive to fall into mi tea."

"Stop messing about," William demanded. "You know full well what I mean."

"Well, actually," Jack insisted, mouth full of Yorkshire Tea-soaked biscuit, "no, I don't. What *do* you mean?"

"This silly driving lesson thing with Joey," William snorted, still in a stew about Jack's offer. "I might remind you, Jack, that Joey is *my* son, and—"

"Then I suggest, Bro, that you treat him like one, before you lose him, too," he advised sternly.

"And by that you mean?" William harrumphed indignantly.

"To put none too fine a point on it," Jack returned sharply, "you almost lost your lovely wife because you couldn't resist sleeping with yon whore Sandra."

"Samantha," William corrected. "She was – is – called Samantha."

"I know what she's called, damn it, William," Jack replied, his anger beginning to rise. "My point is that you have no idea how to keep your most important people close, because you keep making the same stupid mistakes and taking the same wrong decisions. For goodness' sake, don't drive your son away, because, sure as hell, you will if you insist on following this line."

"But, he's too young to learn to drive," his brother complained, now very much on the back foot, "and you are making things worse by your interference in a family matter. Butt out, Jack."

"Joey is almost twenty, Bro," Jack replied emphatically, "and you have no idea how to treat him as such. And, do you know what the sad thing is in all of this? You never have, and you never will. And get this, daddyo, *your* son *will* learn how to drive with me, and you can't stop him. What will you do? Throw him out, just to try to assert your authority? Get real … and grow up."

He slammed down the receiver, fuming at his stupid brother's stubbornness.

"That went well," Jenny said sarcastically, stepping in to his turmoil.

"Yes," he replied, disappointed, "and now, damn it, my biscuit's taken a nose-dive into my tea, which, incidentally, is now tepid. Why I bother I don't know."

He was interrupted by an urgent banging at the front door.

"Val?" he said as he ushered her inside.

"Please, please don't give up your idea about teaching Joey how to drive," she pleaded. "I would much rather he was taught by someone I can trust than by a nobody who will inculcate bad habits into him. His father has refused to pay for him, and, worse, he won't take the time to teach him himself."

"I've just had a serious difference of opinion with your husband on the phone," Jack replied calmly. "I warned him that he would lose his son's respect if he didn't clue himself up, and, do you know, he didn't seem to care. He refused to get down from his high horse and take the sensible pragmatic route. Do I have *your* permission, at least, Val, to teach the lad how to drive?"

"Of course you do," she replied. "I was the one who sent him down to you in the first place, don't forget. *I'll* deal with your brother. Trust good old William to get it wrong again."

"Panacea, Val?" Jack asked with a smile.

"Pana...?" she replied, a little puzzled, until almost instantly she twigged. "Cup of Yorkshire Tea – the cure for all ills. You are the sort of tonic, Jack, that every woman should have."

"Can I take it that William is still not finding it easy to cope with everyday family living?" Jenny asked as they sipped and chomped.

"Not only is he finding it nigh on impossible to come to terms that *all* his children are almost adults," Val explained, "but that you can't *control* by edict. He doesn't seem to be able to learn from those around him."

Her last words were delivered with a gentle nod and raise of the eyebrows in Jack's direction.

"Anybody like a fresh pot of Yorkshire Tea?" Jack offered. "Just off to make missen one. Taking orders. Speak now or forever hold your pieces."

"How's your Jessie getting on these days?" Val asked once Jack had disappeared into the kitchen. "You said she was having a bit of trouble finding her feet at school."

"As usual, Jack solved the problem," Jenny replied, smiling and shrugging her shoulders, "in the only way he knows how – head-on and pragmatically. He really does seem to relish sorting stuff out for other folks. Born to it, I think."

"As he has done with our Joey," Val agreed. "No ifs and buts. Straight in. Problem solved. You are so lucky to have stumbled upon that one."

"Stumbled upon?" her sister said, a half-smile creasing her face. "I've known him almost all my life, for goodness' sake, Val. We were friends in junior school long before I knew anything else really. He used to say that we were having a date when we played together in the playground. He was a strange little boy then, and now he's grown up--"

"To be a strange man," Val laughed, "but only in that he doesn't react or behave as you might expect most *ordinary* men to behave. Not a selfish bone in his body."

"Don't get me wrong," Jenny said, turning half-serious. "He has his moments when he can be a little difficult. Yet, he has that knack of drawing you in to his way of thinking almost without you knowing it, and before you realise where you are – job's a good un. Sorted. Problem evaporates."

"Mi lugs are burning," Jack's cackle burst into the conversation as he backed his way into the lounge with a tray of tea and cakes to hand.

"I see you've found my stash of goodies, young man," Jenny laughed.

"I haven't got where I am today without knowing where I can lay mi hands on cake and stuff to accompany mi Yorkshire Tea," he replied seriously comical.

"Our Jessie is at her friend Jessie's," Jenny finished the conversation. "Been there for a sleep-over. She's really looking forward to next term at school."

-o-

Stick and Joyce's back garden was alive with a huge range of colours, just like their old house in Altofts the first time Jenny and Jack saw it. This was where Jenny got a lot of her ideas for *her* garden. She loved gardening in the spring and adored even more sitting in the sun at the back of the house when everything was in riotous bloom in the summer.

"I like your garden furniture, Joyce," Jenny said, admiring the teak bench, table and chairs.

"Got then last year," Joyce replied, as she sipped her rose hip tea – her latest march towards a healthier life style. Stick couldn't abide it himself, so he steeped himself in Yorkshire Tea and Columbian ground coffee fit to drown in, Joyce would say.

"Did I tell you that I received a telephone call from half-brother Eric?" Jack slipped slyly into the conversation as they watched their children playing happily together.

"You're a dark horse," Joyce said, quickly taking up his little snippet. "Recently?"

"Not really," he replied casually. "Probably a week or two ago."

"A week or…?" Joyce said, puzzled he had waited such a long time to tell her. "How did he seem?"

"A bit rough around the edges," he said, "but really quite pleasant. I didn't tell you because he said they were going away for a bit."

"Holiday?" she asked, not expecting an answer. "They?"

"Honeymoon," he replied, draining the dregs from his mug.

"Well, I wasn't expecting *that*," Joyce replied, taken aback. "Do you know when they're back?"

"Probably round about now, I should think," he said, matter-of-fact.

"Come on, Our Jack," Joyce insisted, shuffling to the edge of her seat. "I know you. You'll have worked it out to the nearest micro second. Give. When?"

"Yesterday at two, into Normanton from Brid," he smiled. "He said he would phone when they'd had time to turn stuff around. Then, Joycey-babes, we'll set up a meeting on neutral ground perhaps. Just you and me and him for a starter, to see how we get on. OK with that?"

"Course I am," she replied. "Meks perfect sense for us to suss out what's what before we widen the group."

"Not sure what I'm expecting, really," Jack added.

"Probably best not to expect too much, eh? And have no preconditions or pre-conceived ideas based on his lineage. Clean sheet and all that for starters, eh? Still not sure what I'm expecting to come of the affair."

"No pre-conceived ideas, remember?" she reminded him as crepuscular night began to usher them inside.

Chapter 11

"And what are you thinking, Our Jack?" Joyce asked, breaking the silence as the car approached the White Swan in Normanton.

"Not sure what to think," he replied almost reluctantly. "Part of me is quite excited, but the other more urgent part wants it over with. Not sure what I'm expecting to gain from … this."

"Open mind don't forget, eh Jack?" she replied, her warm smile reassuring him. "Nothing ventured, nothing gained. He can't be all *that* bad. You sure you know where you're going?"

"Left on to Snydale Road, then right on to Favell Avenue," he said. "Should be there in a few minutes. She said there'd be a blue Ford Fiesta outside."

"She?" Joyce asked, puzzled at the reference.

"Eric's wife, I suppose, as they've just come back from honeymoon in Bridlington," Jack explained, a grin dithering. "She's called Ellen, I think."

They drifted off into their individual silence bubbles, trying to anticipate the greeting they might receive – bonhomie or bombast. Either could be disturbing in the wrong circumstance. If they could survive the first few minutes without rancour or recrimination, then they stood a reasonable chance of establishing some sort of a satisfactory relationship.

"Welcoming party," Jack warned as they pulled in behind a run-down blue car that stood tiredly before a restless profusion of the most beautiful flowers and shrubs they had seen for some time.

"Hello," Jack said to the young lady behind the rickety front gate. "You must be Ellen."

"And you must be Jack and Joyce," she replied. "Related but not to each other. Eric and I have been looking forward to this meeting – me more than him, I have to say."

"Very true," Joyce said, pleased to note that the young lady before her, appeared smarter and sharper than she had anticipated.

"Eric's waiting in t'front room," Ellen added. "This way please."

Jack wasn't sure. This could go either way, although there was no reason, no indication that the outcome would be either black or … white.

"Lovely front garden you've got," Joyce said as they paraded down the path to the only door at the side of the house. "Is the clump by the path alstroemeria and azalea?"

"You know your plants," Ellen smiled. "Indeed they are. I love my garden. I could stay in it all day, which is more than I can say about Eric. He's a practical sort of a chap. OK if you want something mending or altering, but not for planting and growing stuff. I suppose we're a good match, really. Here we are. Please come in."

"As in most good partnerships, perhaps," Jack said as he went in and took off his shoes.

"There's no need to—" Ellen intervened.

"Oh yes, there is," he interrupted. "A man's home is his castle, and I can't be bringing outside muck in."

"It's funny you should say that," she went on, putting on her slippers. "My Eric says exactly the same. Interesting."

"'Ow do," a deep voice echoed from the front room as they walked in.

"'Ow do," Jack replied. "Tha must be Eric. Pleased to meet thi."

"Na, that's a surprise," Eric replied. "Ah dint expect tha'"

"'Ow's that then?" Jack said, surprised by his directness.

"I expected tha'd talk all lardie dah, like," Eric replied, as dour and straight as a Yorkshireman could be."

"Ah wor browt up in Norminton by mi mam and a granddad as good as yer'd find anywiyer," Jack said, keeping his irritation under wraps. "She wor a lovely woman, mi granddad wor an inspiration – but mi fatha wor a arse'ole o' t'worst sort – but then tha'd know all abaht that, si thi."

Joyce cringed mentally at this all-out broadside – not the way to make friends and influence people, Our Jack. She wasn't prepared for Eric's response.

"At last," Eric said, "somebody as I can relate to, as tells it as it is."

He got up from his chair and, moving towards Jack, offered his extended hand in greeting.

"It's rayt good to meet thee, Our Jack," he said, a grin splitting his craggy face. "Tha's welcome in my 'ouse any time."

"Likewise, Our Eric," Jack grinned. "Good to meet thi at last, and, I've got to say, thi lovely wife an' all."

"Jud Holmes, eh?" Eric said as they all settled to tea and scones. "I know 'is lad's lad. Thi cousin … Jack."

That, Jack wasn't *expecting*. His lad's lad? Could this be the missing link he thought he knew about, but couldn't find?

"Thee and 'im could be twins," Eric went on. "As like as two peas, bloody image on each other. Why 'aven't I seen thi before today?"

"A case of timing really," Joyce replied, matter-of-fact. "We didn't know until very recently that you weren't living with your parents, and we hadn't made contact because of them. My mother – *your* mother – left my dad to bring us up on his own, and—"

"Mi mam was mistreated by mi fatha – *your* fatha – and caused 'er a lot of distress when she found out he had fathered you," Jack continued. "We know none of this is your fault, because you didn't ask to be born. Had we known sooner, we would have tried to see *you* sooner."

His voice tailed away into a general all-encompassing buzz of conversation, as Joyce took in their surroundings. Nice enough older house in need of a certain amount of renovation, which, obviously they had started already. Joyce liked Ellen's choice of colour scheme and the alterations that Eric had started to make, showing style and taste.

"Took us quite a long time to get together long enough to want to get wed," Ellen's melodic voice faded back in.

"Choice or external … pressure?" Jack asked, knowing which it was likely to be.

"My mother worn't overly keen on my choice," Ellen said, a defiant smile underlining *her* views, "and Eric senior didn't rate *me* at all."

"That daft bugger didn't rate anything outside on 'is next pint," her husband chipped in with disdain. "So, I wouldn't set too much stall by it. We're together now, and that's all as matters."

He threw a loving look across at his wife which she caught with a happy and satisfied smile. There was no doubt in Joyce's mind that they were perfectly matched, and they knew it.

"We simply nipped out one day to t'registry office in Leeds," Eric explained with a wicked smile, "wi' out parents knowin', and Bob's your uncle, we came back Mr and Mrs."

"Can you tell me summat about mi Uncle Jack's son, Jack, then, please?" Jack asked after a moment's quiet. "Onny, I didn't know he existed until quite a while after mi mam died. She had a photograph in her handbag, and never got around to telling me about him."

"Aye, lad, I can," Eric replied. "In fact, I can do better'n that. Next time tha comes ower to visit, like, I can tek thi to see 'im."

-o-

"Turn up and no mistake, then, Our Joyce," Jack muttered as they turned in to Leeds Road, Methley, on their way back.

"In what way, Jack?" she replied, as she offered him a sucky sweet to pass the time.

"Although I felt there needed to be no pre-conceived ideas about Eric and his bride," he went on slowly, "I found him – them – more amenable and personable than I had expected, and that surprised me."

"I know," she replied, unable to gainsay *her* own feelings too. "I can't say anything about his sire, because I never met him, but young Eric is nothing like my mother. She could be snidy and sharp. I don't see any corners or sharp edges with him. Reminds me a bit of somebody else I know and love."

"Love, Our Joyce?" he laughed. "Does Stick need to worry, then?"

"No, Jack, daft bugger," she laughed. "It's you. He's a lot like you."

"Not as good-looking as me, though," he said, beginning to giggle.

"Don't push it, mate," she replied, grinning. "One compliment is enough in any week."

"Verdict?" he asked, knowing she would give a straight answer. One of the things he loved about Joyce was that she could always be relied upon to give an honest opinion – straight, honest and impartial. *That* was Our Joyce.

"I like them – both," she said unequivocally. "Ellen is

a poppet, with some lovely ideas on décor *and* gardening. Jenny would get along well with her. I'm very glad we decided to try to draw them into *our* family."

Joyce and Jack had always been close. Much closer than your usual friends – more like family. They both knew that each had the other's best interest at heart, and could be relied upon to be there at need, no matter what. He loved her like the sister he never had and would do anything for her. Stick and Joyce were a match made in heaven, too.

"Next move?" she ventured, knowing what his answer might be.

"Leave it to them, don't you think?" he replied, almost evasively. "We've done what we set out to do, and so it's their turn to show they are serious when we are talking about long-term relationships, eh?"

"Just what I thought you'd say," she added, smiling at the clever way he asked questions, so the answers would be present in the question. Obvious, really. The answer was definitely the one you would have given anyway, or so he led you to believe. "My dad would have said 'smart arse', but I think it is clever rather than smart."

"The difference between the two?" he asked, eyebrows raised and smile sneaking through in that challenging way he had.

"Sometimes there is," she replied, "and sometimes there … isn't."

"Smart arse," Jack laughed as they turned into their estate, ready for home, a cup of Yorkshire Tea and a digestive.

"I'll take that as a compliment, Our Jack," she said with a grin as she slammed the car door.

"I'm home!" Jack shouted as he snecked the front door after him. "Anybody available to welcome a weary traveller home from his journeys?"

Chapter 12

August never delivered the sort of weather it was contracted to deliver, with much more rain and many more soggy days on the menu than the sun's comforting warmth. When Jack was a child, folks complained bitterly about the overpowering heat and the dreadful water shortages. Whereas, nowadays nostalgic conversations seemed to turn around those wonderful days past when people conveniently forgot about the difficulties they had had to endure.

Standing in the conservatory watching the rain pounding an already soggy garden, sun-loving Jenny yearned for warmer times when she could sit out and enjoy the warmth.

"Will we ever go to warmer holiday countries, Our Jack?" she murmured, a disconsolate frown descending.

"Isn't this country warm enough for you?" he replied, slipping his arm around her shoulders.

"Warm-ish," she sighed, raising a disapproving brow at the answer she wasn't expecting to hear. "Rain, Jack, rain."

"Aye, but it's warm rain," he laughed, not feeling her disapproval.

"I don't … see … any … sun," she said slowly, hoping her husband would catch her urgency and react accordingly.

"It's probably in Spain," he added quickly, realising at

last she was unhappy at not having the sort of summer she loved as a child, "hotting things up for when we go to visit. How does a week at October break grab you?"

"We can't afford it," she said quietly, looking him in the face directly, never sure what was going on behind those minxy green eyes.

He turned without a word, and left her gazing at the incessant rain, to return within a couple of minutes, a long envelope in his hand.

"Early post?" she asked without blinking.

"It's for you," he replied, a great grin spreading. "Well, go on then. Open it."

"What's this?" she gasped as she tore open the flap gingerly. "Spain? A week's worth of Indian summer sun? You're having me on. Right?"

"No, my little pigeon," Jack grinned. "It's the real deal. OK then?"

"Of course it is!" she yelled, squealing with glee as she threw herself at him. "You lovely man, but how…?"

"Good management," he replied, touching the side of his nose with his forefinger. "It's all sorted. A week's worth of fun in the sun."

"Hang on," she went on, a frown beginning to rain on her parade. "Our Jessie? She's not on the ticket. What--?"

"She didn't want to go," Jack interrupted with a shrug. "Wanted to stay here."

"Like in … here?" Jenny said, puzzled.

"She's staying with her bestie, Jessie, at David and Irene's," he assured her. "They're all happy about it and they're off to Butlin's."

"Wow! You sneaky…" Jenny said, unable to get her head around Jack's subterfuge.

"You don't want to go?" he mocked. "I'll just nip down the road and ask Mrs—"

"You dare, buster!" Jenny said as she threw her arms

around him again and smothered his face with kisses.

"After all," he advised her, "Jessie *is* a teenager, if only in her head, and she does have her own views on most things that bother her. You know as well as I do that she'll be fine – and *no* trouble."

"By the way," Jenny said as she finished mashing a pot of his favourite Yorkshire Tea, "you haven't told me yet how things are with your half-brother."

"Well," he started, once settled in his chair, "where shall I begin?"

-o-

"So, you *were* right," Jenny mused, a satisfied look on her face. "That photo from your Mam's handbag *was* your Uncle Jack's son. Any idea where he lives and who his mother is?"

"We'll soon find out," he agreed, "because Eric knows him, and the next time *we* meet, Uncle Jack's son will be there. Point is, do I really want to pursue it, and will it throw up more questions than there are answers?"

"The only way you'll find out—" she insisted.

"Is to suck it and see," he replied quickly. "I know."

"Door, Jack," Jenny interrupted, as the bell intruded into their conversation.

"There's no need to call me names, Our Jen," he quipped, laughing as he prised himself out of his chair.

"They're both in their rooms, Jess and Imogen Rose," Jack shouted as he ushered his other guests into the lounge. "Go in you two. Just off to put the kettle on. I know, it doesn't suit me at all."

"Irene! David!" Jenny exclaimed, jumping out of her chair to embrace and greet their friends. "Come in and sit ye down."

"You've been living with Jack too long," Irene laughed as she hugged Jenny.

"Good to see you both," Jack added as he took their coats. "Fleeting visit because you were just passing, or you simply couldn't last a moment longer without a cup of my Yorkshire Tea?"

"It's good, Jacky-boy," David quipped. "It's good, but not *that* good."

Seemed like only yesterday they were enjoying each other's company in Filey at the White Lodge.

"Come up on the Pools," Jack went on, "and you've come to share your good fortune with your dear friends and family?"

"They live too far away," David laughed. "So, we came to you."

They all laughed and settled into that easy comfort that comes only with close friendship, camaraderie and family.

"We've come to share a piece of really good news with you," David started, as he sank his teeth into one of Jenny's succulent scones. "The sort of *really* good news that will have you floating back to work next week on a cloud – and before you quip about me awarding you a big pay rise, you'll understand that this news pales *that* into insignificance."

"Well, come on then," Jack replied eagerly, sliding to the edge of his chair. "Spill."

"I hope you haven't found yourself a new job," David explained, fielding a serious look for a change.

"Well, as a matter of fact," Jack replied slowly, equally seriously without blinking as he held his friends concerned gaze., "I … haven't."

"You bugger!" David exhaled loudly.

"And the reasoning behind your question is?" Jack said, a huge grin recognising there could be news he might enjoy.

"You remember we talked about our collective future a

short while ago?" David explained.

"The one where you were given promotion," Jack said jovially, but with the hint of a sharp edge, "and I got the boot?"

"Well, not quite in those terms but … yes," David agreed. "The decision has been taken at a higher level that *that's* not going to happen."

"Not going to…?" Jenny said, puzzled and relieved in equal measures. "How do you mean?"

"Cecil P Barchester *is* coming back," David insisted. "Of that there is no doubt. But … he's not coming back to Broughton."

"Not…?" Jack puzzled slowly. "Then what? Where?"

"You remember where I said I would be going, to allow him to feed back into the system?" David said.

"Cross Flatts Junior, wasn't it?" Jack replied cautiously,

"Well, *he's* decided it will be too much disruption to *our* school," David pointed out, "and so he's decided to take over at Cross Flatts instead."

"Good old CPB!" Jack said, punching the air. "Business as usual then, eh Boss?"

"Seems like it," David replied. "The Old Firm's back in business."

-o-

"You have got to be joking," Jack gasped, Friday evening of their first week back at school after the summer holidays. "How could *that* happen?"

"It's true," Jenny insisted. "I spoke to Val only half an hour ago."

"But, how did that come about?" he replied. "How come? William – a head teacher? What has our world come to?"

"His head," Jenny said, raising her eyebrows. "the lady we met—?"

"Mrs Joan Silvester," he interrupted.

"She's apparently had a fall." Jenny went on, pausing briefly only to take a breath, "and has badly bruised her ankle."

"She *was* a bit stumpy," he added.

"Jack!" Jenny gasped. "Don't be so uncharitable. She's going to be off another week."

"Just saying. A week in which to run both children and school," he sighed, a grin forming. "He'll never cope, you know."

"He may surprise you," Jenny insisted.

"And pigs might fly," he laughed. "He wouldn't know where to start."

"How's my little girl coped this week, do you think, Jack?" Jenny asked tentatively. "She's—"

"Coped very well, Mum," Jessie's little voice piped in from the hall doorway as she floated into the room. "Any chance of a cup of Yorkshire Tea, Daddy Jack?"

"That's ma girl," Jack grinned as he took off to the kitchen to replenish their supplies, every-ready for a cup of his favourite tipple.

"I love travelling to school with Daddy," Jessie continued. "It gives me time to think about what I'm going to do during my day, even when he *will* persist in talking and cracking his weedy jokes."

Jenny laughed, knowing full well what her ten-going-on-thirty-year old daughter meant. As soon as Jack had returned and put down the tray, his daughter flung her arms around him.

"Thank you for everything, Daddy Jack," she muttered as he drew her close. "I love you for what you have done – and I love riding to school with you in our new chariot provided by Grandpa Jim. School's taken on a whole new meaning for me."

"No more bullying for you to sort out in your own way,

eh?" he replied. "More friends to make?"

"I needed only one to start with," Jessie said with a huge smile, "and she's called … Jessie. After that, we'll see."

"This calls for a—" Jenny started, to be interrupted by the front door bell insisting it needed to be answered.

"We come bearing gifts," David's unmistakeable voice filled the hallway as he handed over an enormous bag. "A Chinese from down the road."

"I know they are a shortish race," Jack quipped, "but to be able to fit into a bag of that size?"

"Jack!" Jenny warned with an indulgently nervous smile

"What?" he replied, raising his brows in fun.

-o-

"To what do we owe the pleasure, Cousins?" Jack asked as he munched his way through a large plate of sweet and sour chicken and pork with egg fried rice and … chips.

"I just wanted to say thank you for today," David answered, his napkin tucked into his shirt collar, "and the rest of this week, really."

"I'm the one who should be thanking *you*," he replied, picking pork out of his teeth. "Without your intervention, we wouldn't have had much of a future, and my daughter wouldn't be as happy in school as she is now. *That* means a huge amount to me."

"By the way," David said quietly as they cleared away and washed up in the kitchen. The children were upstairs playing, and Jenny and Irene were enjoying a post prandial coffee in the lounge. "I received a letter from Great George Street, letting me know that the local education authority intends to send in a full team of inspectors to have a look at our practices sometime soon."

"That's all right by me," Jack replied, "as I'm sure we've nothing to hide."

"They said they'd like to watch you teach French to your class of eight-year-olds," David went on. "Would that be a problem?"

"Of course it wouldn't," Jack said, putting on the kettle and opening a bottle of his best brandy – his *only* bottle of brandy. "How many times, during my probationary year, did I entertain HMI and groups of teachers to watch my French lessons, so *they* could learn how to do it?"

David smiled, thinking back to that halcyon time when *this* young man of a mere twenty-one years, with all his bravado and panache, demonstrated his language-teaching skills to groups of thirty or more, with neither nerves nor fear nor hesitation. *This* young man had been one of the first handful of teachers in this country to train specifically to teach French to primary school children. They were the avant garde using their skills with their newly-developed language course – *En Avant* – that had been developed and produced in Leeds by E J Arnold, a Yorkshire educational publisher. He was special, this young man – though it wouldn't do to admit it to him.

"Then we should pass with flying colours," David said, a smile decorating his face. "It's no more than a formality, part of an authority-wide move to check on standards. It will do us – and you in particular – a lot of good."

"You can count on me, mon brave," Jack replied with a salute and a click of his slippered heels.

Chapter 13

"How's your nephew doing, then?" Jenny asked at the beginning of February half-term break. "Going out with him this week?"

"He's almost ready for his test which I have applied for him to take soon," Jack replied. "Why? Want to come out with us?"

"Nothing, really," she said, a wistful look on her face. "Just wondering."

"Come on!" he interrupted. "Out with it. Whenever you wear *that* look, there's usually *some* knotty problem that needs fixing. Holiday in the sun do it for you?"

"How on earth did you work that one out?" she gasped, as he hammered the nail almost up to its head.

"Four words do it, Jenny," he laughed. "The first one's 'read' and the last one is 'book'. It stands to sense. Our week in Benidorm *was* a success, wasn't it?"

"I promised young Joey that I would help him pass his driving test," he added after a moment or two's hesitation, "and we're not too far away from that."

"OK," she replied, "but it's five words."

"I wasn't going to tell you this," he added, ignoring her last comment, "but I've booked for Spain again, in the Whitsuntide fortnight, for … ten days."

"Eek!" she shrieked, throwing herself upon him, which he defended, feeling she might try to tickle him to death.

"You are the loveliest man alive."

"It's onny mi money you want me for," he parried, "and for t''olidays I tek you on in t'sun."

"Of course it is," she agreed, kissing him once again, "but there are *other* things about you I quite like as well, although they'll have to wait until the nippers are out of the way."

"Can't wait," he said with glee. "It's been at least … three days since…"

"All right, all right," she butted in quickly as George William and Florence May bounced into the room. "We'll discuss *that* later."

"How come we can suddenly afford foreign holidays," she asked, "when before it was always Filey?"

"It was easier when the children were younger," he explained slowly. "Hop into the car and – bingo – we were there in a jiffy. Whereas now, what with these new-fangled jet liners and competitive package holidays, it's cheaper and quicker to nip ower to Benidorm. Plus, guaranteed warmth and unfettered sunshine."

"You haven't answered my question," she insisted with a smile. "Thought you were getting away with skirting the part where you have to explain how we … *afford* … *it?*"

"Part of the answer, dear heart, lies in the word *cheaper*," he answered with a touch of sarcasm, "and the fact that I am being paid more now."

"Smart arse," she muttered as she edged closer to him, preparing an all-out frontal assault.

"Mammy?" George's little voice squeezed between them.

"Yes, my little one?" she said, throwing a warning glance at her husband that he had better beware. "What is it?"

Jack slid slowly and surreptitiously off the settee and on to the floor to escape Jenny's glare. Florence May giggled as she watched her daddy crawling along the carpet towards the kitchen.

"May I have a … why is Daddy trying to make himself look like a spider?" George asked, puzzled at his father's strange behaviour.

"Going to make a cup of tea, no doubt," Jenny replied. "Just ignore him."

"Daddy," George shouted in glee, as he leaped onto his back. "Drinking chocolate for me please."

"And me," Florence May added as she crawled along beside him. "Look, Mammy. I'm a spider, too."

They disappeared into the kitchen, leaving Jenny gasping and rolling her eyes in supplication for release to some imaginary deity. She *knew* her Jack loved her and their children, but could she continue living in this cauldron of an emotional wringer? Could she live outside of it, and without the sentiment and physical stability it brought? Would she ever be able to live without Jack? And what about Simon?

She thrust all thoughts to the back of her mind as he brought a tray into the lounge, children behind carrying their empty mugs very slowly and carefully.

"There we are my sweet lady," Jack said quietly as he poured. "You all right? Anything the matter?"

My god! And *she* was supposed to be the intuitive one! It seemed like he could smell even the slightest ripple of discord of anything that wasn't quite as it should be.

"Why?" she replied. "Should there be?"

"That's an answer I would never have expected from you, Jenny," he said quietly, a concerned frown forming. "Is it something I've done – or *not* done?"

"Of course not, silly," she replied, half-heartedly, which Jack noticed straight away, but said nothing.

"If ever you feel like anything different?" he said, nodding towards the tray, eyebrows raised as he poured his favourite tipple, an almost imperceptible confused frown dancing in his eyes. She noticed straight away.

How could she be even *thinking* about anyone else when she had the man of her dreams next to her? Was it the unknown that was exciting her? The complete opposite of what she had? Could she ever *love* anyone else? An almost imperceptible shudder ran through her.

"Someone walk over your grave, Our Jen?" Jack said as he chomped and sipped, aware of a 'difference' around his wife.

–o–

."You can't be serious!" Val gasped at what her sister had to tell her. Val had already noticed a change in Jenny's outward demeanour, slight though it might have been. "The man that most women would give their eye teeth for? He wouldn't be single for long, you know. Trust me."

"I have no intention of leaving Jack," Jenny assured her sister. "It's just that Simon is so—"

"Not on your horizon, my dear," Val warned. "Jack's not stupid by any means, and so unlike any other man I have ever met. He's smart, quick and would sus you out in an instant should you give him cause. Be careful you *don't* give him cause. You never know how he might react."

Her last sentence was delivered deliberately slowly, laced with as dire a caution as Val could muster.

"Are you my sister or what?" Jenny said, taken aback by the severity of her warning. "I've done nothing wrong, I hasten to assure you, and—"

"You never will," Val replied quietly, "because if you do I'll tell your husband immediately. I won't allow you to use and hurt him. I'm sure he won't allow you to hurt him either. I needn't remind you that straying thoughts are all that's needed to sink a thriving relationship. *You* above all should know that. Now, *enough*. I'm going back to my husband, who's not a patch on yours."

The front door clicked as Val made her dignified if indignant way out, back to prepare tea for her thoughtless and ungrateful husband, leaving her sister shell-shocked and deep in thought. Why had she allowed Simon to intrude into her private thoughts and life, for no reason? She had no idea. He seemed to light up her mind when she wasn't expecting it. Fortunately, she had her own Jiminy Cricket that wouldn't allow her to stray – not even in her mind. For goodness' sake, why should she?

Now she felt deflated and degraded and dirty for allowing such thoughts the freedom to wander throughout her mind at will without hindrance.

"Hello sweet lady," a familiar voice broke her free from her introspection. "Lovely to see you again."

"My god!" she blurted out without thought. "Si … Jack!"

"My name *is* Jack," he replied with a laugh. "Thinking of your fancy man?"

"Fancy…?" she answered, confusion blushing her face near-crimson.

"Si…?" he laughed, feeling a little uneasy but not allowing her to see it.

"Sorry," she said, throwing her arms around his neck. "I was miles away."

"Hopefully you were miles away with me," he added, a slight smile covering his disappointment at her slip, "and not with Si."

She kissed him in full-on passionate embrace, designed to reassure him that she loved him, promising more later. Jack wasn't so sure, feeling it might have been a gut reaction and not genuinely meant.

Doubts thrive on such small seeds – doubts that weren't supposed to *be* there.

"Joey's lesson good?" she asked, hoping to divert his

obvious thoughts, though *that* was unlikely. He never forgot an impression. She would either have to tell him, or show him, or both. She knew her Jack, and it wouldn't be easy.

"He's ready for his test which will be at the end of this week," Jack replied quietly. Unlike him. He was never *this* sort of quiet.

"Cup of tea and a biscuit?" he asked flatly, making for the kitchen door.

"I'll mash it," she replied lamely, noticing his flat and un-ebullient manner. This wasn't like Jack. She couldn't do this to him. It was like the joy had just dropped out of his world, and he had become an ordinary mortal. This just wouldn't do. Yet…

Chapter 14

"Calm down, Joey, and take it easy," Jack advised his nephew as they sat waiting in the Test Centre, off Austhorpe Road in Cross Gates. "Don't forget you're an excellent driver who *will* pass. Relax and do what comes automatically."

Joey nodded, focusing his mind and attitude. He was used to the 95 he had been taming over the last weeks and was now ready to show his – and its – worth.

"Mr Ingles?" a deeply resonant voice boomed around them. "This way please. We're going into the parking lot to test your eye sight."

"That's not an English accent," Joey replied, trying to make conversation with an automaton who was not about to trade words with him. The door to the car park closed in on his last words, drawing Jack back in to the nervous chatter within.

He'd been here a couple of times already in recent history, to fail and subsequently to pass *his* driving test. The difference in his case was that he didn't have the luxury of a car to practise on between paid lessons. His driving instructor, Harry Wormold, was a good teacher, but the best teacher in the world is no substitute for lots of hands-on practice.

-o-

Joey and his uncle drove home for the most part in silence, both, no doubt, reflecting on the day's business. They drew up outside Val's and ambled into the house, once again in silence.

"Well Joey," William said, a told-you-so look on his face. "I assume because of your silence, you failed, and—"

"Actually, Dad," Joey interrupted, a self-satisfied look creeping in to contradict his father once and for all, "I passed."

"With flying colours," Jack added, putting a supportive hand on his shoulder, "with an excellent comment from the examiner."

"You clever young man!" Val exclaimed, hugging her son. "I *knew* you would do it."

"I couldn't have done it without Uncle Jack," he said, breaking off to shake his hand. "His faith in me and his patience carried me through. The examiner actually said that he had never had such a good driver in one so young. Thanks Uncle Jack. I owe you."

"You owe me nothing," Jack replied. "It's been a pleasure – and a hoot. You can repay me by chauffeuring me around when I'm too gaga to drive."

Val and Joey laughed as they looked across at William's dour expressionless face.

"I can't afford to provide the finance for you to buy a car, you understand," William chipped in. "So, it's been something of a waste of time, really."

"Actually," Jack butted in, "the agreement was that if he passed his test first time – which a little mouse just whispered that he did – by the end of the coming July, the 95 will be his. This has been agreed between us – Joey, Grandpa Jim and me. I will make sure it's serviced, taxed and has a full tank, and in the meantime, he can keep his hand in by chauffeuring family."

"Yes!" Joey hooted, punching the air.

"And as you are now the extremely advanced age of twenty," Jack added as he made for the door, "consider it a belated birthday present."

"Can I give you a lift home, Uncle Jack?" Joey added with a cheeky grin and a wink. "You're getting on a bit now you know."

"No thanks, old chap," Jack guffawed. "Time enough for that later. 95's not yours – just yet – although you need to come and drive the Old Girl several times every week to keep your hand in."

"Why is it, Mum, that Dad's so negative about everything I do?" Joey said quietly when he and Val were alone in the kitchen.

"I haven't been able to fathom that one out, I'm afraid, love," Val replied, at a loss. "He used to be positive and quite easy to get on with, but, lately…"

"How can two brothers be so different?" he mused. "I mean, Dad and Uncle Jack are poles apart. They don't even *look* like each other."

"Was that Uncle Jack, Mother?" Mary's voice rushed into the kitchen before her body had had time to charge open the door.

"Why do you ask?" Val said.

"Uncle Jack speaks French, doesn't he?" Mary asked urgently.

"Yes, he does," Val replied, somewhat puzzled as to its relevance. "Why?"

"Two new students joined our class towards the end of last week," she went on seriously, "and they're French. I just wanted to be able to … converse better. They're twins."

"That's nice, dear," Val said. "Identical?"

"No," Mary replied, becoming a little impatient, "they're fraternal. Marie and … Pierre."

"What about your French lessons?" Val went on, realising why she needed conversational French so urgently.

"Never take much notice," Mary answered, almost dismissively. "All the teacher wants us to do is pass the silly exam. Not good enough. *Extra* lessons would carry a cost implication as well, you know. Not doing *that*."

"I have no doubt that if you take your need to your Uncle Jack, he would consider it," Val said as she mashed the tea and buttered a couple of scones. "There might be a cost implication, too. He's not a charity, you know."

"Uncle Jack? Charge?" Joey butted in quickly. "Nar."

"Not helping, Joey!" Val added, a stern withering look bearing down on his shoulders.

"Only two scones, Mother?" Mary asked, as she eyed her mother's baking hungrily. "Don't *you* want any?"

Mary laughed at her own joke, that no-one else found remotely funny.

"Cup of tea and scone for Joey and me," Val replied, drawing them close, out of Mary's reach. "You only came in when you heard your uncle's departure and the kettle's being put on."

"But seeing as it's you," Joey added," I'll do you a dose as well."

"And me, please," their brother piped in as he rushed into the kitchen at the vaguest hint of food and drink.

-o-

"Does anyone fancy a run out to Malham tomorrow?" Joey asked once they were assembled in the lounge after their sip and snack. "I'm driving the 95."

"Love to," Val said, encouraging her son to be bold.

"Me too," Ed added. "Have we ever been there? Where is it?"

"Yorkshire Dales," Joey explained. "Never heard of Malham Tarn and Cove?"

"Sis? Dad?" Joey asked.

"Go on then," Mary joined in. "If I *have* to."

"Can't," William answered, not lifting his eyes from his school stuff. "Too much to do for school."

"Can't you just take one day off as the lad's asked you?" Val said, a disbelieving gasp escaping her mouth. "Not even *one* day?"

"'Fraid not," he insisted firmly. "Far too much to do."

"Then I'll ask Aunt Jenny and Uncle Jack," Joey insisted. "We could use two cars and have a picnic."

-o-

"I do hope William's going to be all right," Val muttered as they prepared to set off for the day. Both cars had been packed to the gunwales, with enough food and drink to sustain a battalion of KOYLI. As with many of the February half-term breaks in recent memory, the weather was bright and crisp, promising a glorious day by the time they reached their goal.

"He won't even notice we've gone, Val," Jack replied, a grin inching over his face. "I'll be surprise if he even feeds himself."

The A660 through Otley would no doubt be very busy, with a traffic queue back past the Chevin and on towards the Darnley Arms by the Old Pool cross roads. That stretch of road had the Chevin hill standing sentinel to the left, and a wonderful view over the Warfe Valley to the right, towards Pool in Warfedale and on to Harrogate a few miles beyond. This was a dangerously winding and narrow road with only one quarter of a mile overtaking stretch, where the unwary could be sucked in to a funnel that might seduce them into an unwise manoeuvre, allowing them to complete their journey fifteen seconds sooner.

The country roads from Gargrave and Coniston Cold were too narrow to offer the 'luxury' of overtaking, particularly when a chugging tractor chopped your speed to a yawning amble.

This journey brought back many happy memories for Jack, from the time he and David, with Irene and Lee, had spent a few memorable days in each other's company, travelling about in his pal's apology of a little car. That's where David proposed to Irene, and *he* almost proposed to Lee.

Jack wasn't sure how he would feel walking the same street and climbing the same Cove as he did with Lee. Yet, he was a hard nut to crack, was Our Jack, and he wouldn't show any emotion. *That* was a chapter in another book that would never be revisited. *This* was *now*, with the family he would love and cherish forever, without demure. He had been born to have Jenny and Jessie and little George William and not-so-little Florence May. They were his life, and that would – could – never change.

Yet, there still seemed to be an almost imperceptible difference in Jenny's outward demeanour; a difference that only *he* could detect. He would have to find out what it was, but would this be the right place and time?

-o-

The urgent rattling of the front door letter flap startled William out of his deep thoughts. A sharp glance at the lounge clock reassured him that his family must still be in Malham, or thereabouts.

"Who on earth's that?" he muttered, deciding to ignore their insistence. He couldn't be disturbed as he still had a mountain of work to get through, and even he needed to have a break from school work at some stage.

Realising, when the rattling grew louder, that they weren't about to go away, he prized himself from his chair and shuffled to the front door. He could see through the spy hole in the door that the young man on the step wasn't someone he recognised – at least not visually. Should he open the door? He wouldn't find out if he didn't, and the young man didn't seem in any hurry to leave.

He was tall and slim, with blurred oriental features, although the straight, fair hair raised the suspicion that he was of mixed race.

"Yes?" William said as he opened the door.

"Mr Ingles?" the young man asked in a very polished British way. "Mr William Ingles?"

"It is," William agreed, "for what it's worth."

"My name is William Ng," the young man replied politely, a slight smile playing around his mouth. "You don't know me, but I've been searching for you for quite a long time."

"And," William said, his quiet reply belying his profoundly puzzled look, "what has that to do with me?"

"Well," the young man explained, "I've come from Singapore to find you, because my mother is Susan Ng, and … I … am … your … son."

Chapter 15

"You can't dismiss him as inconsequential and cast him aside because he's 'inconvenient', Val insisted. "For God's sake! He's your son!"

Indignation, disbelief and disappointment swam in her eyes, underlining in her mind the widening gap between them that had recently begun, ever so slightly, to narrow. How could he have done this, when he was on National Service in the Far East, having professed his undying love for her in every letter he sent.

They weren't married. They weren't even engaged. Yet, she felt … betrayed. Again. Would they survive this new kicking he had given her? How many more secrets would squeeze out of the woodwork? Something rotten in the state of Ingles, perhaps?

"How *could* you?" she went on quietly.

"How could I what?" he asked, puzzled at the not-so-obvious question.

"Think, for goodness' sake, man," Val retorted, sharply sarcastic. "I assume *he* wasn't the result of some immaculate conception? Normally it takes two to tango, from what I hear."

"No need for *that* sort of sarcasm," William muttered, eyes downcast.

"There's every need for it," she replied rounding on him viciously. "This is now twice you've let me and our children down."

"But it happened before we were even engaged," he complained, trying to shift the blame onto a perfectly natural occurrence.

"We were together," she insisted. "Do you want me to show you the love letters you sent me? The love letters you sent while you were sleeping around?"

"I wasn't sleeping around," he urged. "It happened only once – a one off that meant nothing to me."

"And that's supposed to make me feel better?" Val answered with a disdainful snarl. "I tell you what, boyo, if I'd known about your whore, I would have had nothing to do with you. Fortunately for *my* children, I didn't."

"Where do we go from here, then?" William asked quietly, lost for an answer to his predicament.

"I assume that that's a desperately rhetorical question," Val answered tartly, "because I don't *have* an answer. There are those sensible people – and your brother and my sister are two of them, I am sure – that would advise having nothing to do with it, or … you."

"That's not—" he started.

"Don't you dare say 'fair', she replied, her anger rising again. "Nothing's fair that you have done since we've been in this relationship. Perhaps Dad was right."

"I don't know what you mean," he said defensively. "Your dad—"

"Had *your* card marked from the start," she added aggressively. "What's the saying? Like father like son? The only good thing to come out of your family is your brother, and he's worth ten of you without breaking sweat. Now, I'm going down to see my sister, and don't you dare follow."

The front door clicked shut under its own impetus as Val strode down the front path to escape from this madhouse of sexual impropriety.

"Cup of tea, Val, and --?" was the greeting as soon as her foot crossed the threshold.

She threw her arms around her brother-in-law, kissed him on the cheek, and sighed deeply as he reciprocated.

"Come on, lovely lady," he said quietly. "Come in and tell me what's up."

"You wouldn't believe me if I told you, Jack," she replied, settling down in the lounge, tears beginning to gather.

"Oh yes I would," he shouted from the kitchen as he mashed a fresh pot of his favourite tipple. "It has to be something to do with yon husband of yours, and, by the sound of it, something serious again like … dare I suggest it … infidelity?"

"You are *so* smart, my lovely man," she replied as he set the tray down on the coffee table, "and my sister is such a lucky woman."

"Come on now," he grinned jovially, trying to lighten her mood. "Who snitched and what do you want, lovely lady? Jenny's just nipped out to take wee Georgie-boy to his friend's house for an overnight stay. Jessie's at *her* friend Jessie's, and Florence May is at your Mam's."

"A decent husband might be a good starting point," she answered, as her latest revelation poured out.

"Why is that no surprise to me?" Jack said once she had finished her tale, a steady flow of tears beginning to underline her disappointment in his historical infidelity once again.

He moved over to the settee and, sliding his arm around her shoulders, he drew her by-now sobbing body to his. Resisting at first, she relaxed slowly with his gently insisting arm offering the solace she desperately needed.

"Why couldn't he be like you, Jack?" she asked, knowing what his answer might be. "Straight and honest."

"He's his father's son, I'm afraid, Val," he replied,

straight as ever, "and I'm *not*. You deserve better, and so you know what my answer to this whole sorry issue would be without asking."

"I know," she said, a deep sigh underlining her reply, "but how can I rid myself of this turbulent man when his children need him, and—?"

"They don't need him as much as you might think," he urged. "For one thing, he's never there – never has been – when they need him, and they *are* now grown up. There's nobody more grown up than Our Mary, and she's only fourteen, for goodness' sake."

The front door rattled, and its oil-less hinges squeaked as Jenny eased her way back into the hall.

"I'll make a fresh pot while you have a natter with your sister," Jack said as he made for the hall door.

"Val," he mouthed at Jenny as he kissed her, and pointed lounge-ward, with a nod and a raise of his eyebrows. "Just off to make a fresh pot."

-o-

"What's he going to do about his bastard, then?" Jack asked bluntly.

"Jack!" Jenny warned.

"What?" he replied, eyebrows raised in that questioning way.

"Not helping," she tried to explain.

"He's right, Jenny," Val chipped in. "Jack's always right, and I've no idea what he's going to do. I don't really care anymore, to be honest. I wish sometimes that I'd taken Dad's advice."

"Which was?" Jack asked.

"Not to become involved," Val explained, "because of his – your – father."

"Sound advice from a wise man," Jack agreed, nodding sagely.

"One thing's for sure," Val added, "his offspring's not crossing *my* threshold again."

"Again?" Jack queried.

"He came while we were in Malham," she explained, non-too pleased at what had happened, "and William invited him in, having no real proof that what he was claiming was in fact true."

"Does he realise the implications of that?" Jack gasped. "I mean…"

"I know," she replied with a shrug and a deep sigh. "He's never been endowed with a great deal of common sense, unfortunately. We're going to have to watch out, I think."

"Any sign of Mrs Silvester returning to school?" Jenny asked. "Recurrence of the ankle injury isn't it?"

"Week after next," Val replied. "William has this coming week, after the holiday, and she returns to take over the reins again. Between you and me, it will not only be a relief for him, but it has cemented in his mind the desire not to become a head teacher. Better be off, as the boys will be back soon, ravenous as usual no doubt, and Mary should be there now."

"Well," Jack mused once his sister-in-law had returned to *her* place, "that's a cough drop and no mistake. William always was a dozy bugger, and even I, as a seven-year-old, could see that. No proof. No corroborating evidence – no sense."

"I hope William sees sense, and doesn't expose his family to danger," Jenny sighed. "You can't be sure with him."

"The only means to go some way to corroborating this newcomer's story," Jack added slowly, "is to use some of the techniques they have of blood-testing, although *that* isn't wholly accurate. Then, there's this new-fangled process that they call DNA testing, I believe. How exact a process *that* is, I've no idea. At least it might be able to rule folks *out*."

"Better not to get to that stage," Jenny replied, a worried look on her face. "Don't you think?"

"It would have been better if William had kept his pants *on* when he was away," Jack harrumphed, a disgusted look adding weight, "especially as he was almost *betrothed* to Val at the time. Out of sight out of mind, eh?"

"Surely he *must* know whether he had his way with this young girl or not, "Jenny added. "Wouldn't he?"

"You never know *what's* going on in *his* head at *any* time," Jack said, getting up from the settee. "Cup of tea?"

–o–

"OK, Class 6," William said at the end of the first day back, "books in desks. Girls get your coats from the racks and line up at the door, followed by—"

"William?" a familiar adult voice broke into his consciousness, driving out his end-of-day routine. "Is it really you?"

William whisked around sharply, not expecting to see the man standing before him, holding a little girl's hand.

"Peter?" William gasped. "Peter Gittins. My goodness, it's been an age. Rebecca *your* daughter? I never twigged the connection."

"She's only just started here," Peter replied. "She was bullied at her last school, and as the teachers did nothing to stop it, I was advised to bring her here."

"Good choice," William agreed. "Look, come through to the office and we can have a quiet chat. Do you live close by?"

"Haw Hill View," Peter replied quietly. "Moved from The Crescent in Altofts so Becky could come here, and then on to the High School next year. Obviously, she hasn't passed her scholarship – yet – but the teachers at her last school said there shouldn't be a problem."

"From what I've seen so far," William agreed, "she is bright – probably brighter than most in the top class."

"Going to have to go," Peter said as he turned towards the door. "Got to find Rebecca because she's got Guides after tea, and—"

"How's Jenny getting on?" William asked as they reached the door.

"Died in childbirth, old chap," Peter murmured slowly, "having our Becky, but that's something for another time."

"Look," William offered, "why not come along to ours on Saturday for the day, and we could have a good old chin wag about … stuff. I'll ask Our Jack and his family to join us, and your Becky could get along with his daughter, Jessie, who's the same age. What do you say?"

"Can I let you know tomorrow?" Peter said, not quite sure how his daughter might take the suggestion.

"Course you can," William agreed as they wrung hands, bringing back memories for both, and closing the office door quietly behind him.

That was an unexpected blow. He had never had much to do with Peter's Jenny, but she seemed to have made *him* happy – and sad at the same time. This brought him back to earth with a bump, making him realise *he* hadn't been the best husband to *his* lovely wife, and father to his beautiful children.

Tears began to well at the thought of the unnecessary difficulties he had dragged her through, causing her needless stress and upset. What could he do to redress the balance? To show her he really did love her?

The journey home was a quiet one, with William struggling to find solutions to several knotty issues. He was reasonably sure he didn't want to be a head teacher – too much like hard work and too much stress. He had had enough of *that* in his life, thank you very much.

How was he going to find the way to resolve the problems he had caused and *was* causing for his wife? If he carried on in his usual boring and indecisive way, he could lose her, and that would push him over the edge.

Joey was now a man who needed some slack to come to terms with his future life. He needed his father's support and guidance, not negativity and aggravation. William had had enough of that with *his* father and needed not to visit that sort of boorish behaviour on *his* son.

The early teenage of an adolescent girl was a place he had no wish to visit, particularly the world within which *his* daughter existed. He needed advice from his wife so that he might negotiate the barriers and avoid the pitfalls that Mary might drop to impede his path forward with her.

"Hello family," he shouted jovially as he snecked the front door behind him. "Anybody like to greet a lost soul who wouldn't mind a nice mashing of Yorkshire Tea after a very busy day?"

-o-

"You'll never guess whom I met today," William said, as he finished his after-dinner coffee in his favourite chair by the luxuriously roaring log-burner that had cost him two arms and half a leg to buy.

The three youngsters in the family had already escaped what they thought might be the fall-out from the usual hostilities between their parents. Mary had an essay to write, Ed physics homework, and Joey applications to write to whichever organisations might offer him apprenticeships in his chosen field.

"No idea," Val replied, almost without interest, as she sat down with *her* coffee, "but I've no doubt you are about to tell me."

She had almost reached the stage where she didn't

care anymore, and whatever he threw at her, she would bat away to the boundary, which he wouldn't pursue.

"Do you remember Peter Gittins?" he asked, looking earnestly into her face which he rarely did of late.

"Of course I do," she replied, noticing straight away his unusual engagement with the conversation. "He was a pal from school and the army that you haven't seen since *we* got together. Married Jenny Vicars, I seem to remember. Why?"

"His daughter's in my class," he replied quietly, obviously moved by what he was recalling.

"And why does that upset you?" Val asked, surprised and concerned because she had never seen him so genuinely upset by someone else.

"Well," he started, "ten-year-old Rebecca has only just joined us – bullying at another school, I believe. The sad and upsetting part is that her mum – Jenny – died in childbirth, obviously not having had the opportunity to know her beautiful daughter."

Tears began to well in his eyes, and Val was visibly moved by his unexpected and out-of-character show of emotion. He paused for a moment or two to regain control of his emotions.

"This set me thinking on the way home," he went on, "how a useless and thoughtless failure I've been as a husband and father, and—"

"William—" Val interrupted.

"No, Val," he stopped her, "please let me finish? I need to engage with my children before it's too late, and to do that, I need your help, because I've no idea how. More than that, I need to show you how much I … love *you*."

She could see how much he was struggling with this out-pouring of guilt, and, more than at any other time in her married life, she realised how important her husband was to *her*. Understanding that this was a genuine cry for help, she sat on his chair arm and kissed him as she stroked his hair.

"You mean it don't you William?" she said earnestly. "You really mean it."

"One thing he said before he left the school," William added as he slid his arm around her, "was that I should be aware of a group of young Malay men, visiting ex-servicemen of our generation, who had spent time in the Far East doing National service. They have been claiming to be servicemen's sons, but it's turned out to be a scam. The worrying thing about that is, how did they find out where we all live?"

Chapter 16

Despite all Val's protestations and worries to the contrary, dinner that Saturday afternoon, was a glorious affair, largely brought about because of Jenny's culinary wizardry. The house was full and rang to the chatter and laughter of children and young people like it had never before.

Mary had secreted herself in her room to await the arrival of one of her school chums, and once the dining room had been cleared and the new-fangled dishwasher filled to the gunwales, William, Jack, Peter and Joey sat in the lounge with George William and Florence May at their feet playing with their toys. Jessie and Peter's Rebecca were engaged in earnest discussions about some serious matter close to their hearts at the dining table.

This allowed the two sisters to spend time in the kitchen out of the way for the time being.

"Is there something wrong with your William, Our Val?" Jenny asked.

"In what way?" Val replied. "There's always been something wrong with him. Why?"

"Well," Jenny began, "to put none too fine a point on it, he looks quite … affable."

"Ah, *that*," her sister said with a smile. "You've noticed."

"How wouldn't I?" Jenny went on. "I mean, he's usually withdrawn and not interested in anything human conversation has to offer. He's even been pleasant around his sons. Joey seems to have noticed the change too."

"Ever since he came back from school last Monday," Val began to explain, "there's been something … different about him, about his attitude towards … everything, really. I think it's something to do with his chum, Peter Gittins."

"Hasn't he said anything about it?" Jenny queried, quite uncomfortable with anything unexplained or puzzling. After all, *she* was supposed to be the intuitive one – the one who was able to explain the inexplicable.

"The one thing he did say, however," Val said dropping her voice almost to a whisper, as she looked over her shoulder to make sure no-one else could hear, "was that Malay son of his probably wasn't blood at all. Apparently, there is a scam wandering around that several of his countrymen have hatched a plot to fleece some of the national servicemen of William's generation. The police have been informed and some of them have been rounded up and corralled pending an investigation."

"Good heavens!" Jenny exclaimed. "They should be dragooned and deported."

"There are moves afoot, Peter says," Val added, "but the one purporting to have William as his sire, can't be found."

"Gone to ground, eh?" Jenny added. "Send in the Jack Russells I say."

"Apart from bringing up a ten-year-old, Peter," Jack asked, "what do you do now?"

"Well," he answered, "I went on to do an engineering degree at Leeds – didn't fancy teaching – and followed that up with a diploma in mining engineering at Whitwood Tech. Didn't fancy becoming a teacher like owd Will here."

"Steady," William countered, "not so much o' t'owd, if you don't mind."

"I was undermanager at St John's pit until it closed in 1973," Peter went on, "and then I became the same at Sharlston."

"Difficult having that job with shift working and bringing up a little un on your own?" Jack said. "I tek mi hat off to you, Peter."

"Aye, it is that," he replied. "Still, our Becky's two nans pitch in, and now we run on well-oiled wheels. Couldn't do it without them. When I'm on nights I don't get to see her very often, but we manage. She's happy – now – and that counts for everything."

"What's your brother, Gordon, doing now?" Jack asked, settling back into the settee. "Med his fortune yet?"

Peter was silent for a few moments, as he screwed his face and pursed his lips in distaste.

"How can I say this without causing offence?" he started. "He and I don't get on. He did me out of a reasonable amount of money a few years ago, and now we don't speak. Haven't done for ten years. Least said soonest mended, I think."

"No chance?" William said. "Not for your brother?"

"Maybe one day," Peter replied, "but not now."

-o-

"It doesn't hurt as much now," Peter said quietly, a far-off look in his eyes, "but it never goes away. I miss her. We both miss her. Although Becky has never seen her, she still misses having a mother who would have loved to dote on her."

"That has to be hard," Jenny said, "and it must leave you treading water to a certain extent."

"True," he replied, "but she's mi life, and I must bring her up as Jenny would have wanted. Who knows what will happen in the future? The present wi a ten-year-old is all I can contemplate and cope wi now. We've a nice two bedroomed house facing the park we allus used to play in as nippers, and we couldn't ask for any more, really."

The house fell silent as dusk began to steal in, slowly filling all the corners from room to room, to the cacophony unleashed on their world by a monstrous murmuration of starlings heading for their roosting sites in the surrounding trees.

"Time's moving on," Peter's soft voice broke the silence, as the logs in the burner cracked, spat and glowed sullenly, creating dancing shadows throughout the room. "We need to be away after a wonderful day, for which we thank you. Lovely grub and fabulous company, it's done us both no end of good."

"Won't you stay for a cup of tea and a piece of cake, Peter?" Val asked.

"Nowhere to put it," Peter laughed, patting his stomach as he stood up, just as his daughter came into the lounge, her arm linked with Jessie's. "Time to go, Poppet."

"Do we have to, Daddy?" she replied. "I like it here. Jessie and I have had a good time, and we are friends."

"We'll have to," Peter said, "because, if you remember, we need to call off at Nana Gittins' to collect our washing and shopping. We have an hour's drive don't forget, and we can come again, can't we Val?"

"Door's always open, Peter and Rebecca," Val offered, "and we will look forward to seeing you again soon."

–o–

"What did you think?" Jenny said over a cup of tea, once their three had been put to bed.

"What?" he replied, staring into their glowing fire as he was about to indulge in *his* piece of cake and cup of Yorkshire Tea. "Peter?"

"Among other things," she said, smiling at his eagerness not to let his cake go stale or his tea freeze over.

"Well," he started, to be interrupted by the urgent rattling of the letter flap.

"Yes?" Jack barked as he opened the door on a tall dark-skinned young man of about twenty. "What do you want?"

"Mr Ingles?" the young man said, quietly surprised, taking one step backwards.

"Who wants to know? And does he owe you money?" Jack replied, a threatening scowl warning the young man to be quick as he had a rapidly cooling mug of tea waiting to be drunk.

"My name's Jack Ng," the young man responded as he flashed a dithering smile. "I believe you had a relationship with my mother in Singapore about twenty years ago. You are my father and I am your … son."

"Twenty years ago?" Jack guffawed. "Let me see. That would have made me about … ten. Wow! Some performance for a ten-year-old, don't you think?"

The young man took another uncertain step backwards, a seriously confused look overtaking his face.

"Jenny!" Jack shouted over his shoulder. "Call the police and an ambulance! This young man is going to need both in the next minute or two."

The young man took two more steps backwards before turning and moving off down the street rapidly, coat open and flapping in the cool night air. He understood perfectly where *that* was leading. Jack simply stood and chuckled to himself.

"Who was that, Our Jack?" Jenny said as he latched and locked the door.

"Some cheeky young foreign-looking bugger peddling goodness knows what," he replied, a smile lingering. "Now, where's that cake and tea?"

"You'll probably need to warm your tea up," she said, knowing full well what his reaction would be.

"No fear!" he harrumphed indignantly. "A fresh pot is what's called for. None of your wattered down muckment, thank you very much."

"The police just phoned me," William's voice crackled in the receiver. "Said they had apprehended a young Malay matching the description I had given. They said he was muttering something about a white man with a funny accent who threatened to put him in an ambulance, and could he request political asylum."

"I've no idea where he got *that* idea from," Jack laughed. "There are some unpleasant people about these days. So, you don't have a son from Singapore anymore? Shame. I was looking forward towards a family visit over there. They say it's warm and the food's … different."

"Joking apart, Bro," William's disembodied voice echoed, "that's one worry less."

"Worries?" Jack scoffed. "With a lovely wife and family like yours? You don't know you're born."

"That's just it," his brother urged. "It's because they're so wonderful that I do worry. Later."

Click. Gone.

"There's something strangely different about our William, Our Jen," Jack said, puzzled by the conversation he had just experienced.

"Different?" she replied, curled up in her usual corner of the settee. "How?"

"He called me 'Bro'." Jack puzzled, "and he's not done that for years."

"Perhaps he's growing up at last," she offered, "and realising he has a wonderful brother whom he needs to enjoy."

"I don't know," Jack said. "There was something strange in his tone – something … normal."

"Well, I'm off to bed," Jenny said, yawning and stretching. "I feel like a nice, long, warm—"

"Sleep?" he butted in, a knowing grin developing.

"Aye," she added. "That as well."

-o-

Sunday morning thrust itself upon them, thick and white.

"Daddy! Daddy! Quick! Come look," two ear-shattering voices urged either side of his head on his pillow.

"What is it my little urchins?" he gasped as the weight of two little bodies crushed the air out of his lungs. "Is it the end of the world? Has someone stolen all the grass? Has somebody—"

"It's all … white," George William gasped in awe at what he saw, leaping back to the bedroom window.

"Been out with a huge white paint brush?" Jack continued, as he joined them to look out.

"What is it Daddy Jack?" Florence May asked as she had seen and heard big sister Jessie do on many an occasion. "Not seen *that* before."

"It's called snow, my poppet," Jack explained, "and it's very cold."

"Snow good if you want to keep warm, then, Daddy Jack," she replied with a snigger and a giggle.

"I saw what you did there," Jack said, bursting into a belly-splitting guffaw. "That's very clever. That's ma girl."

Jenny smiled, loving the way he had with their children. He would spend endless hours with them, making them feel good about themselves, and having fun, stopping only when they had either had enough or when it was food time. He loved his children and would do anything to make them happy and secure.

"Shall I tell you what we can do after breakfast?" he whispered conspiratorially as he gathered them to him.

"What, Daddy Jack?" they both whispered back, equally secretively.

142

"Then, away to get dressed, washed, and teeth brushed," he went on, "and I'll tell you … after breakfast. Scoot."

They both peeled away from him and hurried back to their bedrooms to make ready for an exciting day ahead. Every day was exciting when they had Daddy Jack at home to themselves. They knew there would always be something different and special to do when he was here, and they couldn't wait until after breakfast to find out what he had in mind.

Chapter 17

Mid-term Monday school day was always a disappointing time in the Ingles household, particularly when Florence May and George William had had their Daddy Jack to themselves for the whole weekend. This Monday was doubly flat and uninteresting because the day before's snow had almost gone, leaving only vestiges of the things they had built in it. Distorted and disfigured snowmen sadly slid away as the temperature rose and the sun's fingers poked them in the eye and swiped away the carrot noses.

By the time school pulled them away from the warmth and comfort of their weekend jollity, all that was left in the back garden was several piles of rapidly melting snow, dotted with pebble eyes and twiggy arms. Still, snow people weren't supposed to last forever, were they?

The return to his Normanton school was a double-edged sword for William. He wasn't looking forward to the traipse through the snow, but he was quite elated that Mrs Silvester would be returning after her accident, lifting the weight of headship from his reluctant shoulders.

Day light was only just beginning to sneak into a cold forbidding world as William drew into the make-shift carpark of a school that was built long before cars had appeared to make working life less parochial. The carpark's compacted earth and stones made a reasonably hard surface – until the frost melted … and it started to rain. No such worry this day.

The sharp, mean lights peeped out from behind the school's huge arched windows, daring passers-by to drop in and suffer the consequences. Fortunately, it was a little too early for the few passers-by to risk it. It was important for entrants to coke-fired schools like this, that were built, on the whole, in the latter part of the nineteenth century, to become acclimatised to their cooler-than-normal interiors.

This didn't concern William one little bit, because all *he* wanted was to survive the day, and return home to continue rebuilding relationships with his family.

His brother, on the other hand, not only loved his family time – he always had – but his working life and the folks he worked with excited him. His journey to school had recently become easier too, with the installation of 'bus only' lanes at peak morning and early evening times, allowing him to cut his bus travel by ten minutes overall. This was not allowing for the ten minutes added on to everyone else's travelling time though, along with the congestion caused by the reduction of the number of lanes along Scott Hall Road's dual carriageway in to town and similarly along the one-way streets into City Square.

The first day back after the weekend always seemed to be overcast, dull and dreary for William, but light and bright with the sun dying to shoulder its way through the clouds for Jack.

Yin and Yang. Opposite, contrasting parts of *one* family.

-o-

End of *this* day saw Jack driving his daughter home in the back of the Rover 95, his friend Stick by his side. They had exchanged pleasantries as Jack had picked him up at the end of Old Lane, and now his hidden worry about his wife forced its way to his full consciousness. Who or what on earth was 'Si', and how could he find out without asking Jenny?

He had this gnawing feeling deep inside that told him that something wasn't as it should have been, and this Si was at its core.

"You all right, Jack?" Stick asked as they approached King Lane-Ring Road roundabout. "You've been very quiet."

"Busy day," he replied, as he climbed out of his reverie. "Looking forward to a rayt good sit down. You?"

"Same," he replied. "Easter can't come soon enough for me. This job doesn't get any easier, Old Chap."

"We're home!" Jack shouted once inside his hacienda, where all troubles fell away and normality enveloped all who entered. "Jenny!"

Strange. No answer. She was usually all over him at the mention of his name.

"Mum's not in, Daddy Jack," Jessie called down from the landing after dumping her school stuff and changing quickly into 'home' clothes.

"It's all right, Sweetie," he shouted back. "kettle's on and I'll just –"

He was interrupted by the click of the front door latch as its Yale key sought to allow access to whomever was outside.

"Jack!" Jenny's flustered and breathless voice jumped at him as his wife hurriedly shut the door, once the youngsters had shot past her and reached the top of the stairs.

"Jenny," he replied softly, a puzzled look on his face. "I've put the kettle on."

"I'm sorry I'm late," she said, a slight flush infusing her face. "Got talking and didn't notice the time."

"Simon?" he asked quietly, a quizzical raising of his

eyebrows indicating his concern as he turned towards the stairs.

"Jack, I…" she started, a look of fear in her eyes – fear that she had let thoughts of this unknown man wander through her mind too frequently. Fear that he was intruding into *their* life like he shouldn't have been.

Jack threw her a sad and disappointed look as he went up to change, a slump in his shoulders telling her he had worked it out, like she knew he would.

"Jack," she went on as she followed him into the bedroom.

"How long, Jenny?" he asked simply. "Have you…?"

"What?" she asked, though with no conviction, knowing full well what he meant.

"Come on, Jenny?" he asked, that quizzical look dominating his face. "How long have I known you? Have you been … intimate with this man?"

There you go – straight to the point. Nail on head. No beating about the bush.

"Why would you think that, Our Jack?" she gasped. "No. Of course not."

"Then you *do* know whom I'm talking about?" he answered quickly. "Who *is* he, Jen? Do I need to be worried?"

"He's nothing to me, Jack. Honestly," she replied quietly, stroking his arm gently. "I met him one day when I was waiting for Jessie outside the school, and—"

"*That* long ago?" he said, a surprised catch in his throat betraying his emotion. "Wow. I noticed a change in your attitude both in general and to me in particular some time ago, but now…?"

"Change?" she puzzled. "How?"

"Full details?" he asked. "Or just in relation to me?"

She remained silent, eyes downcast and filling. What had she done – could have done – to this man who gave everything and did everything to make her and her children happy, and for whom nothing was too much trouble. *She* recognised they hadn't been as intimate as usual for quite a while, putting it down to pressure of full-on family life. Perhaps she needed to rethink, regroup and redirect.

"Jack," she said quietly as she drew him to sit on the settee in their bedroom, "nothing's going on with this person. I just got talking to him – a single parent since his wife died – and it struck a chord. That's all. Perhaps I have been a bit distracted, but I promise nothing's going on – or would there ever be. *You're* my man, and I – we – couldn't live without you."

"OK," he smiled, having sorted *that* out. He believed and trusted her – always had, always would. What she said was good enough for him, but he had to clear the air. "I'll just nip down and mash that tea. Gagging."

"Then gag on this first," she said quietly, drawing his lips to hers in a full-on passionate kiss that held an important message to him – something to be explored when the children were in bed.

-o-

"Message on the answer machine," Jack said as he sat down with his tea and nibble, "from Ellen, wanting to know if we might get together soon."

"Perhaps we ought to invite them over here," Jenny suggested. "A get-together with Joyce and Stick and all."

"Sounds like a plan," Jack replied, his usual smile recording his usual pathetic joke. It wouldn't be Jack without them, Jenny thought. His trade mark. "I'll give Joyce and Stick a bell now to see if we can get a time and date sorted out."

"OK," Jenny agreed, although with a certain degree of reluctance in her mind. She had heard a lot about this Eric and his sire, but hadn't met him, and now, here she was, agreeing to host the most talked-about road show in their existence. It might have been better if she had gone with Jack and Joyce to meet 'Our Eric' on their turf first.

She would have preferred to meet Simon.

Why would he persist in flooding her mind when she had promised Jack…? Indulging in this fantasy, she felt like a naughty school girl sneaking thoughts about some crush she had just taken on. No-one could stop her, because she wasn't doing anything wrong. She could guarantee Jack would never entertain such thoughts, which now made her feel disrespectful, unclean, and … unfaithful. Her naughty secret that had to *remain* secret.

A flush settled in her cheeks again as she could hear her husband on the phone in the hall.

"That sounds great, Joyce," she heard him say. "I'll let them know. Speak soon."

The ominous click of the receiver settling into its cradle warned her of Jack's imminent return.

"Thinking about Simon again?" he said quietly, noticing how uncomfortably nervous she seemed to be as he came back in to the room.

"Simon?" she replied, slightly nervous as she began to lie to him for the first time. "Of course not. Why would you think that?"

"I'm off to make a cup of tea," he said, ignoring the lie they both knew she had told him. "Want one?"

Why did she feel she had to lie, he thought? Not bothered too much that she had broken her promise, but to lie? Should he brooch the subject and confront her? Not worth the aggravation – and then she would know how he felt.

"I owe you an apology," he offered as he set down the tray of tea crockery on the coffee table.

"Apology?" she replied, puzzled at his statement. "What for?"

"Your thoughts are your own and nobody else's business," he went on, "and you should not feel you have to explain where your private thoughts might take you. I won't embarrass you again."

That made her feel even worse. Had he done that on purpose to make her feel bad, or…? Ridiculous assumption. Jack would not – could not – do such a thing. She didn't even know this … Simon. Yet, if he was nothing to her, why couldn't she stop thinking about him? She knew perfectly well the result of such a liaison, and she wasn't even going to give that mind space. Jack loved her without question or condition, was always considerate, and gave her what she wanted and needed in their love-making. She couldn't contemplate being without him, and that's what would happen should she allow Simon into her perfect life.

Once they had finished their tea, she moved towards him, but noticed an almost imperceptible stiffening of his body as she touched his hand. This saddened her.

"Jack," she sighed deeply, reaching out to him.

"Don't worry," he said quietly, moving away slightly. "I'm all rayt."

-o-

"I've noticed a slight stiffening of your relationship with Our Jack," Jenny's mum pointed out one Saturday they were spending in Flora Mae and Jim's company. Jack, Jim and the children were outside playing on the back lawn which was almost football pitch size but bowling green flat and smooth. Little George loved a hoof around with his Grandpa Jim, and *he* wasn't too precious about its use as a playground. 'It's a lawn,' he would say, 'and as such, somewhere for young'uns to … play and explore.'

"How do you mean, Mum?" Jenny replied, feigning ignorance but knowing perfectly well what she was getting at.

"My dear," she emphasised, a self-satisfied smile on her face, "I'm your mother, and if there's anyone in the world more intuitive than you, it's me. Now, tell me."

Ever mindful of the proximity of her family, Jenny's story was short in the telling. Expecting a stern rebuke from her mother, Jenny sat at the kitchen table with a self-pitying sigh, a China cup of tea to hand.

"Just before I married your Dad," Flo started, "I fell for a gloriously handsome young man called Charlie. He was perfect in every way, or so I thought, and I couldn't get him out of my mind. I was sorely tempted to call off the wedding and run away with Charlie. Your grandma – *my* mother – sat me down and urged me to run with my heart, when I had expected her to remonstrate, tell me to grow up and out of my fairy tale fantasy. Needless to say, I settled my mind out of the clouds and my feet firmly on the ground by marrying your dad, and I never regretted it for one second. We had our moments, but, overall, it was the right choice.

"Jack is your soulmate – a perfect man in every way, who loves you to distraction and would give up everything for you. However, if you hurt him with this … Simon, he will never forgive you. Do you want to throw away everything on a whim? I suspect not. Whatever fantasy you want to indulge in – fine – but don't let it creep out and spoil what millions of women would give their eye teeth for, because snap him up they will. Now, reality check and cup of tea time."

Jenny thought deeply on what she had said for a while, until the noise of children and men invading the house brought her check on reality out into the real world. She smiled when she saw George William on Jack's back and Florence may on Jim's. Jessie wandered behind, reading a book – like she always used to do – as she walked, her sixth sense making sure her fifth sense wasn't scrambled by bumping into a wall.

She realised suddenly that fantasy was no substitute for the real world and some imaginary Tom, Dick or Simon was no match for what she enjoyed now, no matter how beautifully appealing he might appear to be.

"Hands washed, you lot," Nan Flo ordered. "A cup of tea first and then George's favourite dinner – cabbage, sprouts and ... liver."

His 'Yuk' of disgust said it all, as everybody, including Jessie, laughed at the face he pulled, knowing full well that *that* would never happen.

"I don't like cabbage an' sprouts an' liver, Nana Flo," George grimaced, "but I *do* like roas beef an' chicken an' … an'… chips!"

"Then, how about roast beef and Yorkshire pudding and roast potatoes?" she offered, knowing what he liked best.

"Followed by some of your bootiful appleses pie?" he added, clapping his eager little hands. He still had a bit of a difficulty with some of his letter combinations, but *he* knew what he meant.

Chapter 18

"**B**loomin' 'ummer!" Eric gasped as he drew on to Jack's driveway, his brand spanking new, bright red Vauxhall Chevette gleaming in the late morning sunshine. "Ah niver expected a nouse like yon."

"I told you!" Ellen retorted, a great, satisfied grin dominating her face.

"Welcome to mi casa," Jack's voice surrounded them as he helped his new sister-in-law from the car. "Our home is your home. I like the car. It's a sight better than my owd Viva."

"Yon 'ouse is a cracker, Brother," Eric boomed as they shook hands and headed to the front door where Jenny was waiting to greet them. "*I* want one o' these."

Ellen punched the air and said a silent, mouthed 'Yes' to emphasise how long she had been trying to get him to shift his backside out of the dark depths of 1920s Normanton and into a modern – preferably detached – 1980s house with all mod cons in the suburbs, somewhere, and she had just the place in mind.

"An' all these bootiful young uns?" Eric went on, enthralled. "Are they all youers?"

After all the introductions, a cup of tea and a piece of Victoria sponge, the youngsters shot off to do their things – Florence May with Valerie, and George William with Billy. Jessie was in *her* room already with her friend

… Jessie.

"Are *you* planning to have a family, Eric?" Jack asked his half-brother as he polished off his last piece of sponge.

"Er…" he stammered, looking across at Ellen for a yea or nay.

"As it turns out," Ellen replied, straightening her frock and sitting back into the comfortable settee, "I have some good news to tell you all – including my Eric."

His face caught one of those 'rabbit-in-the-headlights' moments that none of those present would ever forget. Saucer-like eyes and a deeply furrowed brow left them all in no doubt that *this* was the first he had heard of her 'good news'.

"What's tha mean by that?" he gabbled, with no idea what she was about to spring on him.

"Come on then, ar lass," Eric burst in after a few moments of stunned silence, "don't keep me in suspenders."

"You, Our Eric, are going to be a … daddy," Ellen said quietly, a satisfied smile on her face. "There."

Eric remained in stunned silence for a few minutes, a look of panic and pain vying with happiness, with his mouth gaping and his eyes dancing from side to side seeking support desperately.

"This means…?" he gasped.

"That you're going to start a family of your own," Ellen replied, beginning to giggle.

"Start?" he asked, a puzzled frown not knowing whether to stay or give way to elation and joy. "Does tha mean … we might be 'avin' … more?"

"It does that, my lad," she laughed. "Ifn tha behaves thissen."

They all burst into laughter and bouts of congratulations and slaps on the back for Eric, and hugs for Ellen. Now he *was* confused because he had never experienced such family emotion and such unbridled joy before. By eck!

Was 'e glad 'e 'ad discovered these 'ere relations. No more isolation. No more boorishly negative reactions from parents 'e didn't seem to belong to. Jack and Jenny and Joyce and Stick. Oo wooder thowt it? A real family at last.

"Well done, my son," Jack gushed, wringing his hand warmly.

"This calls for a yooge celebration," Eric boomed, coming to life at last, a yooge grin splitting his face.

"Don't dish out yon cigars just yet, Our Eric," Ellen advised. "There's still a way to go."

"Does tha know," he started slowly and deliberately, "that I've been thinking like perhaps we owt to find summat a bit bigger to live in now that we're abaht to be three – and maybe … fower a bit later, like."

"And I've just the place," Ellen added, a look of smiling triumph on her face. "Ash Gap Lane. Does tha know where that is, Our Eric?"

"Er," he hummed and hawed for a minute, "is it darn yon snicket just past t'Town Hall, top er t'High Street?"

"That's the one," she replied, triumphantly.

"But," he said, scratching his head, puzzled at the reference, "they're all owd 'ouses as we can't afford, and it's on a 'ill wi'out a med-up road."

"Next time you're up there," she explained, "as you step off t'pavement in t'corner – *into the unknown* – have a look at the sign on your way to the tunnel under the railway lines that teks you to Altofts."

"What abaht it?" he said quickly. "There's nowt else dahn thiyer, is the?"

"Building a small estate of *brand-new* houses, my dear," she went on. "Some on 'em are to be detached, and that's what I want. Fancy a look tomorrow? We do need somewhere *decent* for your son or daughter to live in. Don't you think? Somewhere wi' a big garden where they can play in safety wi'out worrying about falling ower and grazing knees on t'cobble stones we 'ave now. Eh?"

-o-

"She's clever is that one," Jack murmured to Jenny as they prepared a tray of tea and coffee and buns. "*He* stands no chance, poor sap. Although it seems like he has picked the right one for guidance. He won't go far wrong."

"They'll be all right together, Our Jack," Jenny replied just before she took the tray into the lounge. "Bit like you, really. Just a bit … different. He's a bit of a rougher version of … you."

"What are you trying to say?" he laughed.

"Did you ever think of becoming a teacher, Ellen?" Jack asked once they'd settled with their afternoon drinks and nibbles.

"Funny you should ask that," Eric interrupted. "We've known each other since secondary school, and in them days it wor all she could talk about. Her one goal in life – becoming a teacher to yon little bairns in primary school. 'A calling' is what she said it wor."

"Then, why isn't she doing that now?" Stick asked, as he wiped a few Victoria sponge crumbs from his mouth corners.

"Does she take sugar?" Ellen butted in, much to Jack's amusement and Stick's puzzlement. He too laughed once Joyce had explained the reference.

"So, why?" Ellen replied, a sad tone setting an edge to her voice. "Mi mam was on her own – mi dad had died from pneumoconiosis – throughout mi schooling, and despite me getting eight GCEs I had to leave school at sixteen to earn. It was a very sad day when I had to give up my aspirations because of circumstance. Still, needs must when the devil calls."

"What about now?" Jack cajoled, testing the water of her resolve. "You could do it now."

"Too late," she sighed. "Too old."

"Not so," he explained. "Bretton Hall College, Wakefield, runs courses for mature students to train as teachers – no age limit."

"Nar," she replied, hesitating as she thought. "I'm –"

"Ey, daft bugger," Erice butted in, "listen to 'im. Ifn there's any chance o'followin' thi dream, tha's got to do it. Can tha find out a bit more, Our Jack, like? If there's any prospect, I'll tek 'er thiyer missen. After yon bairn's born, of course."

"Consider it done, Eric," Jack replied with a grin and a nod. "She'd mek a grand teacher, whether she teks sugar or not, and I know several schools in *this* area that would snap her up."

–o–

"Do you think that Jack was just saying, about me being a teacher?" Ellen asked her husband on the way home after a wonderful day with their extended family. "Onny, I've never heard of this Bretton Hall place."

"Tek 'is word, lass," Eric replied. "He's in t'business, and 'as bin for some years. 'E's sharp and smart, is yon lad, and ifn 'e says it, tha'd better believe it."

"But what do *you* think about it?" she said, after a mile or two's silence. "You know, me being a teacher?"

"Tha's allus wanted to be one," he replied quietly, patting her on the knee as they drew into their street. "So, why doesn't tha tek it on board, stop bleating, and gerr on wi' it?"

"I tell thee what," he offered as he parked outside their house and turned off the engine. "How's about ifn next weekend we traipse across to 'ave a look at t'place? I'm sure Jack will have found a lot more by then, and then tha can mek up thi mind. 'Ow's that sound?"

"Thank you," she said, clapping her hands silently,

a huge grin growing. "You're a good man, Eric Ingles, despite what anyone else might say."

"That's a back-handed compliment, if ever I saw one, and no mistek," he said, bursting into peels of laughter as he linked her arm down the path to the side door. "What a day this 'as bin eh, Ar Ellen."

"Told thee tha'd no need to wyther thissen about thi new-found brother," Ellen said, holding his arm tightly. "I like them. All of 'em."

"Is tha off to tell thi mam about yon bairn yet?" he asked, snecking the door behind them.

"Not yet," she said quietly. "I need to think on it a bit longer. There's another eight months before I'm due, and we've a lot to think on and to do together. All rayt?"

"I love thee," Eric said quietly, on the spur of the moment.

"Did thy just express thy undying love for me then, Our Eric?" Ellen said, surprised at her man of scant emotions. "Wonders'll never cease!"

"Talking to Jack 'as med me realise that it's all rayt to have emotions occasionally – not *too* often like," Eric replied.

"You've really latched on to him, haven't you?" she said, a surprised raising of the eyebrows signalling her feelings.

"He's a rayt bloke," Eric replied. "A lot like me. Calls a spade a spade. Dunt get much better than that."

-o-

"I didn't expect them to be like *that*!" Jenny said once their guests had left.

"He's definitely nothing like his mother," Joyce observed sharply.

"Nor his fatha," Jack agreed. "They are actually a lovely couple."

"Are you sure about Bretton Hall?" Stick asked,

changing tack slightly. "Onny, I've never heard about mature student courses, neither there … nor anywhere else for that matter."

"Neither had I," Jack added, "until last weekend's Times Ed bulletin. So, a few weeks has taken us from having too many teachers to having, magically, too few. I'll find out more about the courses it offers, next week."

"Where is it, Jack?" Joyce asked. "I've never heard of it."

"As far as I am aware," Jack began, "it was a country house in West Bretton, near Wakefield, which was turned into teacher training college in the late forties by t'West Riding's Chief Education Officer, Alec Clegg. I'm not sure about what courses it offers but, as I said, I'll find out in due course."

A rattle at the front door drew Jack into the hall while Jenny and Joyce went upstairs to the children.

"Val! William?" Jack said, glad to see the one but surprised to see the other. "Don't just stand there. Come in. No children?"

"Both Joey and Edward are old enough, of course, to look after their sister," Val laughed, "but she's not there. Something about a sleep over at her friend Aurelia's place. I don't know. Children, eh?"

"Would that be coffee or tea?" Stick asked, popping his head round the door from the kitchen. "Just making a brew. Any takers?"

"Dad's been rushed into hospital," William said, as soon as everyone was comfortably nursing a steaming cup and its inevitable accompanying cake. "His chest, I'm afraid."

"And that's supposed to lead me into mourning, is it?" Jack replied, as he polished off both cake and tea, making sure no crumb was left a-wasting on his plate. "Don't forget, Bro, that he has sucked on those dreadful white

Woodbine sticks for the best part of forty years, so there's no wonder his chest's playing him up."

"Same compassionate young bugger as ever, eh Jack?" William scoffed, taking joy from standing the high ground.

"Look William," Jack hissed, rounding on his brother, "even his other son can't stand fatha's unpleasantness, and feels nothing for him. Tends to underline my views rather nicely, don't you think? Been to see him in hospital, then?"

"Well, er," William replied, trying to evade his brother's inevitably clever reply to no avail, "no, not really."

"Then don't preach to me about that compassion crap," Jack harrumphed, his broadside chopping him off at the knees. "When he shows care for others, I'll show care for him. Or maybe not."

"You mentioned your half-brother," Val mumbled through a mouthful of her sister's excellent lemon drizzle cake. "Have you seen him, then?"

"Left for home just before you arrived," Jack replied, as Joyce cast him a slightly concerned glance. "I didn't think William would have been interested, based on what he said the last time *that* subject was broached. They are a really lovely couple."

"Couple?" William puzzled.

"Aye," Jack continued, a self-satisfied smile gracing his face, "soon to be three."

Joyce smiled inwardly at the clever way Jack had stitched his brother up. He was a lovely man, was Jack – slow to anger, but once riled he was so sharp, Paris's Place de la Concorde guillotine couldn't have done a neater job.

"Will we get chance to meet them any time soon?" Val ventured tentatively.

"It's all up to your husband, Val," Jack batted the question straight back at the server. "I'm sure they'd be delighted to meet *you*. A word of warning though. Eric doesn't get on with his – our – father, and so might not take kindly to a eulogy about him. He's been brought up in a very unloving family environment and has only just found that which he lacked from birth, with his wife, Ellen. You'll like them both – for very different reasons."

"Apparently," Jack went on after a moment's pause to finish off his second mug of tea and his second piece of lemon drizzle cake, "we are quite alike."

"Another smart arse, then," William muttered under his breath which only Jenny caught in passing, causing her disquiet and more than a little annoyance. Her head advised her to keep her counsel, but her heart favoured a swift retaliation. Her private battle was won by a short head only, promising but a brief stay of execution.

"Did he mention anything about your Uncle Jack's son?" Val asked. "You know, about meeting him?"

"Very briefly said he was on to it," Jack replied slowly. "Something about Cousin Jack seeming somewhat surprised, not knowing anything about such a relationship. Said he would have to talk to his mother first. Sounds like he's not been told."

"What's all that about?" William asked, finally waking up to smell the coffee – fresh ground, next to him on the coffee table.

"Keep up, William. Keep up," Val cajoled her husband. "Remember your Uncle Jack who was shot down in the last war? Your mother's brother whom she spoke about often? Our Jack discovered he had a son called … Jack. The strange thing about this, apart from your uncle neither knowing nor even seeing him, is that your half-brother, Eric, *knows* your cousin Jack. Still following? Confused?"

"And what's all this got to do with me?" he harrumphed dismissively.

"Well, *there's* a lasting and telling comment on the importance of family, eh William!" Jack guffawed, casting aside his brother's apathy. "I never thought I'd see the day when your insularity would distance you from your own flesh and blood."

Chapter 19

"What does tha mean, 'e's thi brother?" he said. "Tha doesn't *have* a brother."

"What does *thy* know abaht *my* family, owd cock?" his friend replied. "Of course 'e's mi brother … cos I say so."

"Tha might be spinnin' me a yarn," he said, grinning.

"When were t'last time thy knew me to lie?" his friend harrumphed, putting his pint down slowly on the White Swan's bar counter.

"Aye, all rayt then," he said, a defensive hands-up showing his agreement. "I'll gi' thi that, si thi. All rayt, tell me more."

"Well, for a start off," his friend began, "'e's t'image o' thee. In fact, 'e could be thi twin."

"'As than gor a photo?" he asked, becoming more intrigued as the conversation progressed.

"Nay, I 'aven't," his friend said, "but 'e's got one o' *thee*."

Silence dropped like a brick, hitting the water surface of his mind, sending out concentric rings to the outer reaches, seeing *now* that what his friend was saying might carry a grain or two.

"But, 'ow—?" a puzzled frown creasing his brow.

"'E says it came from *'is* mother," his friend butted in before he had had the chance to finish his question.

"'Ow on earth did *'is* mother get a 'old of *my* photograph?" he added. "And who is *she* when she's all there?

"She's not anymore," his friend explained. "Died a year or two since, but *she* was your dad's sister – or half-sister to be exact. Same mother, different father. In fact, your grandma died only a short while ago, but your granddad's been gone some years."

"Now tha's got me completely flummoxed," he gasped

"The chap in question is called Jack Ingles," his friend continued, "and he's not only your cousin, he's my half-brother as well. So, in a roundabout sort of a way, *we're* related too. How bizarre is that?"

Eric laughed as he looked Jack Holmes straight in the eyes.

"Bloody 'ell!" Jack uttered, a nervous laugh rolling round his throat. "Family just—"

"Got bigger?" Eric interrupted. "I know the feeling well. Same 'appened to me just a short while ago wi' mi 'alf-brother … and your new cousin, Jack, and my 'alf-sister, Joyce. Enuff to send you gaga."

"Hmm," Jack muttered. Did he really need all the hassle an extended family might bring, or would it be good to have another in the family to remind him of the father he never met? "Half-sister? Joyce?"

"Don't ask," Eric grimaced, shrugging his shoulders. "I'll explain later."

"It'd be all rayt ifn I had a photo to 'elp me along," Jack muttered as he finished his pint and wiped his mouth on his sleeve, in time-honoured tradition as Eric made to leave.

"Tha's got one," Eric replied. "All thy 'as to do is look in t'mirror ivry day, and thiyer thy 'as 'im."

The evening air felt chill around his neck as the keen breeze took away the cosy after-glow of the White Swan and its beer, thrusting him into the reality of his trudge home. He hoped Ellen was all right, as she hadn't been feeling particularly well for most of the day. Morning sickness, or summat like she had said, he supposed. Why 'morning' sickness when it usually lasted most of the day?

Queen Street was almost deserted, with heavily laced and curtained windows keeping out the dark and preventing their artificial light from escaping completely. So, he decided to head down Snydale Road with a swift right into Favell Avenue as quickly as the pavement and his tired feet would allow, the evening air dispelling all memories of the one pint he had played with in Jack Holmes's company. This one visit to the White Swan he had made for two reasons – it had always been Jack Holmes's local even though he now lived on Woodhouse Mount - three doors from the corner snicket to Goosehill Fields - and opposite the Hark to Mopsey! He wanted to smooth the path for the two Jacks to meet, but now he wasn't so sure it had been a rayt good idea,

The house was eerily quiet and dark as he unlocked the door and felt for the light switch, a vaguely puzzled frown and feeling of unease descending.

"Ellen!" he called. "I'm back. You in there?"

He closed the passage door quietly behind him as he realised she might be asleep. Though at half past seven that might be a bit of a stretch.

"Bloody 'ell!" he yelled as he saw her prostrate body on the floor of the front room. "Ellen?"

He flung himself down beside her as a weak groan fell out of her ashen face. He made her comfortable before deciding he needed to call Dr Twist. Dashing to his next-door neighbour's, he asked Mrs Grimshaw if she would keep an eye on his wife while he shot off on his bike to the telephone box where Garth Avenue ran into Dalefield Road.

-o-

"But will she be all rayt, Doctor?" Eric persisted. "I thowt she wor a gonner."

"She will be fine, Mr Ingles," Dr Twist replied, a benign smile reassuring him. "She's been overdoing it a little, I fear. That's all. A few days of bed rest and she'll be as right as rain. Will you be able to…?"

"More than mi job's worth," Eric replied, shaking his head. "Symptom o' t' times when you can't get a day off to look after t'nearest and t'dearest, eh? Any road, her mam onny lives on Dalefield Avenue, round t'corner, and so she'll be able to keep an eye. She'll mek sure she keeps her feet up for a bit."

"Any further problems, Mr Ingles, please let me know," Dr Twist advised sternly. "OK?"

Eric thanked the doctor for his time and efforts as he showed him to the door.

"Bloody 'ell, Ellen!" he exclaimed as he carried a tray to her. "Tha gev me a rayt fright thiyer. I thowt I'd lost thee, and what for, eh? Trying to get Jack Holmes to seeing his cousin, Jack Ingles."

"It would a' med no difference if tha'd bin here, daft bugger," she insisted a wan smile dithering around her mouth.

"But ah could a' sin to thee sooner," he replied, wagging his finger at her, "and tha wouldn't ave"ad to spend all that time on t'floor."

"Don't thee wag thy finger at me, Eric Ingles!" she exclaimed in mock seriousness, smiling at his attempt to appear officious and in control.

"Tha could a' deed while I wor aht," Eric said quickly, a look of serious worry in his eyes, "and then where would I a' bin?"

"Tha would a' bin teken up by somebody as dunt know thee," his wife laughed. "Though I have no idea where tha'd find somebody like that."

He wrapped his arms carefully around her as if he was afraid she might break, and kissed her tenderly.

"Steady on," she giggled, "anybody'd think tha wor going to get emotional – anybody as didn't know thee. Tha can 'old me properly, si thi. I'm not going to fall apart."

"Another cup of tea then?" he asked tentatively, with some semblance of an expectant look raising his eyebrows.

"Aye, go on then," Ellen replied with a knowing smile, realising he had his eye on one of yon scones she had baked the day before. Ee eck! Eric wor getting more like his brother Jack ivry day!

-o-

"And can I assume you're going to meet your cousin Jack?" Jack Holmes's mother, Elizabeth asked, impatient at her son's shilly-shallying. His dad wouldn't have hesitated for a moment. He loved his big sister, Florence May, and would have loved to have been part of his nephew's life. She had met Flo several times and had abhorred how her husband treated her. Elizabeth's Jack had wanted to sort him out good and proper, but *she* had counselled caution and not to become involved. Flo idolised her brother and insisted *her* son should be named after him. It seemed, as little Jack was growing up, he began to develop many of the traits his uncle bore, uncannily. This didn't bother Eric senior, because he was convinced little Jack wasn't his anyway.

"I'm not sure whether I can be bothered with all this family stuff, anyway," he replied through a yawn. "Father's not here and never has been – not for me at least. So, why should *I* bother with *them*?"

"Selfish young bugger," Elizabeth harrumphed indignantly at her son's apathy. "You might look like your father, but you sure as hell are nothing like him temperamentally. I for one would like to meet this Jack

Ingles, partly to see if he's any more like your father than you are. I'm just wondering if I've been bringing up a changeling all these years. Dear me!"

Her son raised his eyebrows, shrugged his shoulders, and took his leave – better things to do, like melding his arse to a White Swan stool. He was her son, but still something of a disappointment to her. She shuddered to think what his father would have made of him. She loved his father with a passion that had never faded over the years and *that* marriage wouldn't have changed. He had always talked about the white-walled cottage he would have built for her and a fairy-tale wedding to go with their fairy-tale home.

–o–

"Got my arse on two saddles here, Stick," Jack said as they disembarked the 225X in City Square on their way to school, Monday after an excellent weekend.

"How do you mean?" his friend queried.

"Jack Holmes still hasn't made any move towards meeting me," he replied, "but apparently his mother has – asked if she and I might meet. Failure followed hot foot by success, of a sort."

"I suppose you need to ask yourself what you are hoping to get out of such a link," Stick mused. "Brief meeting to register a further family link, or long-term relationship?"

"It's another line of my family that needs to be explored and cultivated," Jack said with conviction. "There is so much I don't know and would like to find out about somebody who has played such a large part in my life without being alive even, and whom I've never seen."

"My stop I'm afraid, Jack," Stick said as the bus slowed on its approach to Old Lane.

The new car park at Broughton Primary School seemed unusually busy, with more cars neatly parked than the school had teachers. Jack knew perfectly well, too, that a significant proportion of its teachers either had no car or came, like him, by public transport.

"Have we just had an influx of extra teachers," Jack asked, a mischievous grin on his face, "or has a coach trip missed its turning?"

"A word, Jack?" David's voice drew his attention as his head appeared at the staffroom door.

"Visitors, Boss?" Jack said as he snecked the door behind him.

"Do you remember those authority inspectors I told you about a while ago," David asked, "that never turned up?"

"I do indeed," his deputy agreed. "Have they only just arrived because they got lost?"

"Is there anything gets past you?" David observed, a grin beginning to form. "They turned up a quarter of an hour ago, without a by your leave kiss mi … Anyway, do you have any French lessons today? Only, I'd particularly like them to see that if poss."

"I have four," he replied, rubbing his hands in glee and grinning. "Two Year 3s, a Year 4 and a Year 6 – two in the morning and two in the afternoon. Usher them in my direction and I'll give them some lessons to make their little eyes water and their gobs to be well and truly smacked."

"Good man!" David chortled, knowing what Jack's French lessons would do for the school's reputation. "They're in my office now – six of 'em – supping my tea and scoffing my biscuits."

"Those biscuits I knocked on the floor on Thursday of last week?" Jack laughed mischievously. "You will have noticed that I haven't been eating them lately, and that's not because I am on a diet."

David giggled giddily on his way out. Good old Jack.

He *knew* he could always rely on him.

-o-

"Thank you for coming everyone," David started at the hastily convened staff meeting. "I know it's the end of Friday and you'd like to start your weekend sooner rather than later, so I'll be brief. I have just had the preliminary report from our inspectors about our performance over the last few days, and the news is very good. They consider we are performing well, and they have seen some all-round excellent lessons. They would normally have returned to finish off observations next week, but for two reasons they decided they had seen enough – the first reason being the wonderful interaction between pupils and teachers, and secondly, Jack wore them out, craftily 'obliging' them to do group work with the children when they were in his lessons. He has been designated now as our new secret weapon. I feel confident that because of our new nuclear-tipped missile, we will not be receiving any more visits for some *considerable* time. Good Old Jack! And thank you all for staying."

Calls of 'hear hear' and strains of 'For he's a jolly good fellow' accompanied the shuffling of chairs as they vacated the premises – rapidly – to start their weekend.

"Well, Old Chap," David went on, slapping Jack on the back, once the room was empty, "you certainly carried out your threat to give them something to talk about. There was a suggestion from Mr Atkinson, who, as you know, is Inspector for Modern Foreign Languages, that they might like to use *you* as their new ambassador for teaching French to juniors. If that were the case, the school in general – and you in particular – would get an enormous amount of Kudos and not an insubstantial amount of extra cash for equipment and the like. What do you say?"

"Whatever you say, Old Man, is good enough for me," Jack replied, a grin splitting his face.

"How about coming over to ours tomorrow for the day?" David suggested. "The nippers would enjoy getting together and so would we. It's been a while."

"Sounds like an excellent plan," Jack agreed. "How about lunch time? We'll bring the food."

"Wonderful," David said, their conversation trailing away as they made their way towards the carpark.

Crepuscular evening was beginning to draw a darkening veil over the township as parents and children alike bustled about, wrapped against the chill. Only a very few of the hardiest plants had decided it was safe enough to venture one or two pale vulnerable-looking shoots into the cold air to try to hurry spring along, knowing well what would happen should the tail end of winter snap back.

Chapter 20

"Well," Jack gasped as he replaced the telephone receiver, "that was a surprise and no mistake."

"Who was it, Sweetie?" Jenny shouted from the kitchen. "Anybody important?"

"Jack?" she repeated urgently when he hadn't replied, bustling into the lounge to find out why.

"It's all right," he said as she sat down on the settee next to him. "I caught it first time. Just digesting what I heard."

"Which was?" she insisted patiently.

"It doesn't seem like my cousin Jack will be making contact," he explained. "That was his mother, Elizabeth."

"His mother?" Jenny replied, puzzled. "But…?"

"How did she get our number," he said, shrugging his shoulders, "and why has she phoned?"

"Well … yes," she agreed. "We don't know her, do we?"

"Not yet," he replied, "but she's asked if she might be able to see us sometime soon. So, I've arranged it for Saturday, if that's all right with you?"

"I'm not doing…" she started, to be interrupted by a heavy banging at the front door. Throwing Jenny a seriously puzzled look, Jack ambled from the lounge, to be met, on opening the door, by two burly policemen flanking a young boy.

"Mr Ingles?" the taller of the two asked. "I—"

"Why have you brought my son here?" Jack asked urgently. "Where's his mother and why isn't he with her?"

"We are simply the messengers, sir," the policeman replied. "The lad's mother has been rushed into hospital for emergency surgery and the lad has two choices – care or you. Which is it to be, sir?"

"Has he any clothing, personal effects, or other stuff?" Jack asked, puzzled.

"He has a bag that's still in the car, as we didn't know which way you might want to play it," the policeman replied. "You never know in this sort of situation."

"How long is his mother to be in hospital?" Jack asked.

"Long enough for the lad to be homeless unless you decide to take him in … sir," the shorter, balding policeman said in a guttural, non-English sort of a way, as his eyebrows moved slowly up his forehead.

"*Will* you be taking him in … sir?" the original officer asked without emotion, as if he was simply going through the motions. "Or will we be taking him to social services where *they* will look after him until—"

"Certainly not!" Jack interrupted sharply. "He's my son and he will stay here for as long as he needs. Thank you, officers. I'll take it from here."

Jack closed the door once the boy was inside, his bag at his feet, and the police car had disappeared down the street.

"Who are you," the boy asked, a perplexed look haunting his face, "and why am I here? Would you take me back to my mother, please?"

"Who was that, Jack?" Jenny asked cheerfully as she reached the bottom of the stairs, jerking to a halt as she saw her husband with a boy who looked remarkably like him. "And this young person *looks* like he might be your son, Sam."

"Who are you, please mister," the boy asked again as

he sat down in the lounge, not sure what was happening to him, "and where is my mum?"

"She's been rushed into hospital, poorly," Jack started to explain, "and because you have nowhere else to go, and I *am* your father, the police brought you—"

"But you're *not* my father," the boy butted in, tears beginning to well in his eyes. "He's dead. My mother told me when I was … younger. She said that *that* was the reason we had to go to Canada to live with my Grandpa Ron, because my father had left us with no money and we couldn't afford to live here anymore. I don't remember much of all that because Grandpa died, and we had to come back here. Don't know any more."

Jenny turned to Jack, a profoundly shocked look overtaking her eyes. Jack silenced her approaching response with a raised eyebrow and a slight inclination of the opposite side of his head. They needed to attend to the urgent essentials, like finding him somewhere to sleep and to soothe his anxiety of being thrust into the company of complete strangers.

–o–

Although Jessie complained mildly, Florence May moved in with her to allow Sam to sleep in her room. They reassured him that all would be well, but he obviously still had reservations about having his mother replaced by alien folks about whom he wasn't sure. His father was dead, wasn't he? His mother had said so. His Grandpa Ron had said so, and he trusted his grandpa.

If this man *was* his father, then why hadn't he seen him before, and why had his mother lied to him? This Jack person *had* seemed genuinely surprised to see him when those policemen called, *and* he genuinely seemed to know him. This was a very puzzling and confusing world he had strayed into, and no mistake.

Jack had already phoned David about the situation so that he would cover his class for the day – at least until he had sorted things out with the boy.

"Where's your school, Sam?" Jack asked. "I think we ought to let them know, maybe?"

"School?" the lad replied, genuinely surprised at the idea. "I don't do … school. Mother teaches me at home and has done ever since I was old enough to learn to read or do sums."

An awkward and embarrassing silence surrounded them, quietly ambushing the adults like a stealthy assassin, effectively killing their already stilted conversation.

"At home?" Jenny asked, unsure about the implications of such a system she had not heard of before. "What happens when you need to learn about such things as, say, French or science or … I don't know … history?"

"Mother was a school teacher before I was born," Sam began, slipping into an easy explanation, "and she was – is – able to teach me all the things I need and enjoy doing. She does all the teaching, and I do all the learning."

"Interesting," Jenny said, intrigued by this concept of learning, bringing the whole 'Give me a child until he is seven' teaching back to her from university days.

"Well, I won't be able to teach you, my boy, Jack interrupted, "because I will have to go back to work tomorrow – to earn money so that we all can live."

"No," Jenny said, a self-satisfied smile growing, "but *I* can."

"Jenny?" Jack asked, a questioning raise of the eyebrow and a commensurate inclination of the head heralding his scepticism.

"And where are your studies?" she continued.

"My books and things are at home in Roundhay," Sam replied simply, "and I have a … key."

"Are you sure about this Jen?" Jack said, not so

convinced that it was such a good idea.

"Of course I am," she replied, willing to give it a try. "We can't do nothing, letting the lad sit around all day twiddling his thumbs, and besides, it could lead *me* into doing something worthwhile as a job. We have no idea how long his mother will be incapacitated, and so surely it would be better to use the time he is here productively. Don't you think so? Surely you, of all people, Jack...? As well as academic learning there's all sorts of other, everyday stuff he would benefit from learning. We'll nip down to Roundhay tomorrow, when you're back at work and the kids are off to school."

"If that's what you want, Our Jenny?" Jack agreed almost reluctantly.

"Do you think you might bring me home an exercise book or two from Broughton tomorrow?" she asked, excitement beginning to overcome the daunting prospect of trying to teach a nine-year-old boy the sort of stuff he would find useful. The plans were already beginning to form in her mind, as a smile began to grow.

-o-

"And I can't thank you enough," she said, "for taking him in and for looking after him."

The ward was shrouded in that quietly busy noise all hospital's have in abundance, that draws outsiders in at visiting times, releasing and spitting them out at their end.

Leeds General Infirmary was one of those mid-Victorian town centre institutions that provided a modern uptake on the good care offered to all-comers, no matter their state or demeanour. There were areas that needed upgrading and modernising, but the same could be said about countless similar hospitals in many city centres.

"How long will it be now, Lee?" Jenny asked, genuinely concerned that her son was missing his mother.

"Probably a week or so," she replied, "but if it's too much—?"

"Nonsense," Jack butted in. "Jenny has taken a great deal of trouble to continue Sam's studies, so he didn't become bored, and he seems to be enjoying the experience. What do you say, Sam?"

"I like history, because Jenny likes history," Sam began, dour but excited in his own way. "We do a lot about kings and queens of England. It's good."

"He soaks up knowledge like a sponge, really," Jenny added, "and is a pleasure to work with. You see, history was my main subject at university, with a particular interest in the monarchy since 1066—"

"William, Duke of Normandy, descended from Rollo, a Viking who became first ruler of Normandy," Sam interrupted quickly so as not to leave out a single historical fact about him. "William the Conqueror's father was Robert the First, Duke of Normandy, and his mother was Hedeva. They weren't married. William married Matilda of Flanders in the 1050s. He was a contender for the English throne because he was the first cousin-once-removed of Edward the Confessor. On his deathbed *he* promised the throne to Harold Godwinson, but William was having none of it, so he invaded in 1066 – and the rest is history."

"That's exactly what we are talking about," Jenny explained, laughing at his funny, though it was more of a statement of fact than amusing to Sam. "It doesn't take much for him to assimilate his historical interests."

"I taught a lad at Moor Secondary School," Jack added, "who bore very similar traits, only his special knowledge was in languages. On a trip once to London with the school, he went missing, only to be found a quarter of an hour later on Regent Street, giving precise directions to a German tourist … in German … how to get to the

Tower of London. Amazing, and he was only eleven – the student, not the German tourist."

"So," Jenny asked, genuinely puzzled, "isn't that sort of thing *usual* in children of that age?"

"Just think back to me as a child, Our Jen," Jack suggested, a wry smile growing. "How often did I say and do stuff that was strange to other people? You weren't in my class at junior school, but Joyce could tell you a thing or two. *She* sat next to me for most of my schooling there. Although I'm not in Sam's league, the signs were there – not understood, but there."

"Can we go home now, Mum?" Sam asked, a painful imploring expression jumping into his face. "I still have my key, and so we could go home now, if you want. Please?"

"I'm afraid the doctor said that I will need to be here for a few more days," Lee replied quietly. "You like being with your father, don't you?"

"He's all right," he said without hesitation. "but, unlike you, he's not in during the day."

"It's called 'going to work' I'm afraid, Old Chap," Jack explained through a wry smile. "You like Jenny though, and the things you do together, don't you?"

"They're OK," Sam said, after a little thought, "but it's not the same. She's not my Mum. No offence."

"None taken," Jenny smiled. "I can go with that."

"Can we have a quiz about the monarchy when we get back, please?" he added, with a faint twinkle in his eye.

Sam had always done as she had asked without demure or any ostensible relish, but Lee had noticed a slight wrinkling of enthusiasm around his eye corners she had rarely seen before. Perhaps friends were right. Perhaps he should be exposed to a wider – chosen – society? Perhaps his extended family was the ideal she *should* espouse? After all, Jack *was* his father, and he did love them both when Sam was born. Thoughts of 'what if' crowded her mind.

Unfortunately, she had allowed her family to intrude into and to sour the lovely relationship she had shared with a true and loving man. What if…?

"Do you think we ought to make tracks?" Jack asked quietly. "We don't want to tire you, Lee."

"Would it be all right if I had a few minutes with my son, alone?" Lee asked. "Some things I need to ask him about."

"Of course," Jenny replied, nodding to Jack to make a move. "We'll be in the corridor."

"I wonder what she's saying to him?" Jack muttered as they rounded the second double set of swing doors into the cool corridor beyond the cloying disinfectant-infused ward.

"Nothing we need to know about, Our Jack," Jenny advised. "We've become involved at need, and rightly so, but I think you should be prepared to return to the status quo once she's out and back on her feet. In fact, I wouldn't be at all surprised if she took him back to Canada."

"No skin off my nose," he replied, that set look invading his face, telling the world he didn't care a toss, when she knew differently. "I have family that loves me for what I am, not for what I can give. If *they* shoot off to Timbuktu, then that's their affair. If they want to stay, equally, no business of mine."

They stood around for a while, amidst a motorway of trolleys laden with patients in varying degrees of accepting and stoical distress, the swish of stiff starchy uniforms the only noise apart from the oil less rattle of malfunctioning trolley and wheelchair wheels.

"OK, Sam?" Jack said as the youngster sidled through the doors, causing them to swing wildly as his grim face told of the dissatisfied mind behind the tight-lipped façade. "Ready for off? Time for some grub, eh?"

–o–

"A troubled young man," Jack said as he sat with Jenny once all the children had been tucked away for the night. "I wonder—"

"Not for us to wonder, Our Jack," Jenny advised, recognising the distress he was obviously feeling. "She will do what she will do, and we won't be able to stop her. We need to take things as they come, really, I think. We have *our* family to look to."

"Always the intuitive and pragmatic one, eh Jen?" he replied quietly, for him. "But always right. I feel I ought to be there if needed, but want to return to the status quo, to get back on with *our* life. Good call, my lovely. Good call."

They settled back into their relaxed comfort, a cup of Yorkshire Tea and one of Jenny's delicious scones to hand. She felt, however, that there was an air of disquiet about and around him. She couldn't quite put her discerning finger on it, but she felt sure she would be able to cope with it and help him through anything that might surface, whatever it might be.

Chapter 21

"This coming Saturday," Jenny announced out of the blue as Jack was dunking his digestive, and reading the Evening Post on Monday evening, shortly after breezing in from a hard day at the chalk face.

"The coming Saturday, what?" he asked, almost absent-mindedly, neither stopping his dunking nor trying to find words greater than two syllables in his paper. "Don't know why I buy this rubbish," he continued, folding the paper and throwing it onto the floor.

"The day we are going to see your Aunt Elizabeth," she replied, an eye-rolling sigh showing her frustration. "Remember? Cousin Jack Holmes' mother?"

Jack thought for a moment, trying to remember when it had been arranged, but without success. His non-committal shrug prompted her to tutt her annoyance.

"What?" he said in that way he had of shrugging off any blame for a forgotten arrangement, a smile fading away when he saw Jenny's look of disappointment and frustration. "I didn't know we'd arranged to see her yet. Did I?"

"Oh yes you did," Jenny exploded. "Sometimes you can be *so* irritating and infuriating, Jack-No-Memory-Ingles!"

"Come on then, Our Jenny," he said after a few moments of quiet thought, giving her chance to collect *her* thoughts. "What have I done to upset you *now*? Somebody you met before I came home?"

"What do you mean by that?" she replied, aggressively defensive. "Who could I possibly have—?"

"Come on!" he countered, his sharp answer boxing her in. "Never met anyone by the name of – Simon?"

She fell silent, caught between a rock and a hard place, not really knowing what to say that wouldn't incriminate and inflame. She should have known better than to try to outfox and outmanoeuvre her husband. He had been brought up in the midst of conflict all his life, and now *this* conflict could be the one to end them all. What should she do? Try to wriggle her way out? No. He would know straight away. Be honest, and tell him? That would be better but would have the same net result. She would earn his respect but lose him as a husband.

"Shall I tell you what *I* think, my sweet one?" Jack said, knowing that his clever, intuitive wife would guess where this conversation was leading. "Shall I tell you what I think the problem is, and why you are annoyed with *me*?"

Jenny flopped into the chair opposite his seat on the settee, shoulders slumped, face downcast, and tears welling in her eyes.

"I know you love me, Jenny," he began slowly. "You always will. You know that I love you, and that won't change. What you don't know is whether I will stay should you be unfaithful with this … Simon. You see, I've known about your platonic dalliance with him since that last time he was broached."

"But I—" she tried to insist.

"You *have* spent time with him, despite promises otherwise," he interrupted calmly, "albeit in Florence May's playground as you waited to pick up the children."

"How—?" she asked, tears by now drifting slowly down her cheeks.

He touched the side of his nose with his forefinger to

let her know he wasn't about to tell her – yet – but said nothing.

"I haven't so much as looked at another woman since we've been together," he said. "Haven't wanted to, and it pains me to know that obviously I am not enough for you anymore."

"But you are, Jack," she insisted urgently, sliding to the edge of her seat, wanting to be next to him, to reassure him.

"I just need to say one thing to you," he replied, holding his hand towards her, flat palm facing outwards telling her to stay in her chair. "I feel very sad to have to say this, but, if you decide you must take this relationship further, I promise I *will* 'persuade' him not to trouble you again, and I *will* make other living arrangements."

"Jack!" she gasped, sobs beginning to convulse her body. How could she have allowed *this* to happen, to bring *their* beautiful relationship to the edge – her lovely man whom she had always loved, and who had loved her unconditionally in return. Val's words flew back into her mind.

"I won't mention it again," he said, "but, then, I've said that before. If you do decide that you want him more than you want me, you *will* break my heart, but you won't get a second chance."

-o-

"Are you sure you want to come with me?" Jack asked his wife as he readied himself to set off to meet his Uncle Jack's lady. He was a little nervous, which was unusual for him, but that wasn't about to spoil this event he had been anticipating for long enough. "I mean, you don't have to if there's something else you'd rather be doing, like seeing a friend or friends?"

"That was unfair and unnecessary," she harrumphed

quietly.

"Joking, sweetie, just joking," he said as he laughed at her stiffly solemn face.

"Of course I should like to come with you," Jenny replied, low key. "You're my husband and I love you."

He still wasn't sure about the depth of feeling her protestations carried, but it would have to do – for now anyway.

"I don't think you've been down here before," Jack said as he turned right, off Church Road into The Crescent by St Mary Magdalene Church. "Elizabeth lives up here on the right."

One of the more exclusive areas of Altofts, The Crescent had evolved from the1940s into a collection of gloriously chic, well-constructed semi and detached houses set in generously-sized plots of land. Most people's ideal home environment, for the most part.

"Lovely garden, Aunt Elizabeth," Jack said, greeting her at the front gate. "I have no idea what most of these plants are, although my wife Jenny here, probably does. Lovely to meet you at last."

"My God!" she exclaimed, a hiss of surprise escaping her lips. "You're more like my Jack than his son, who, I am sorry to say, didn't want to be here. Says he's not interested in family, although I think he's afraid to meet you."

"Afraid?" Jack asked. "What is there for him to be afraid of?"

"You, my dear young man," Elizabeth replied quietly after a moment or two's thought. "I've heard you're not the easiest person to get on with."

"It's all lies I tell you!" he laughed, genuinely amused by the thought.

"He says things as he sees them, Elizabeth," Jenny piped in, "and some folks feel uncomfortable with that."

"Man after my own heart," the older woman pointed

out, "and there's nothing wrong with that. Just like your Uncle Jack, Jack."

"What *was* he like Aunt Elizabeth?" Jack asked as he warmed his hands on a goodly-sized mug of Yorkshire Tea. "I mean, I know what he looked like – I've only to look in the mirror for that – but what was he like as a person? I would dearly love to have known him."

"For a start off," she began, a wistful look invading her face, "he was his own man who couldn't be diverted from any decision he had made and wouldn't take no for an answer. Recognise those traits, Jack?"

"Hmm," he replied, feeling these comments to be a bit closer to the mark than he had anticipated.

"You see," she went on, "even though your mam was from a different father, the one common factor in *their* lives was their mother – your Grandma Marion. She was the one with definite views and attitudes. They inherited *their* character traits from her, and their personality was influenced and moulded by her. This may sound strange but you, young man, are as much a victim of this outlook as they were. This is why the three of you are so much alike."

"I knew I shared a great part of mi mam's outlook and personality traits," Jack said, sighing as he sank into the settee, "but I never realised mi Uncle Jack would have been part of it, too."

"The only break in yon chain," Elizabeth pointed out with a resigned sigh, "is your cousin – my son – Jack. His father would have been very disappointed in how he's turned out, but then, one of his favourite sayings was 'Tha'll niver mek a silk purse out on a sow's lug oyl.'"

"So, Aunt Elizabeth," Jack asked, desperate to know more about this remarkable couple, "when did you two meet?"

"Saturday 8th October 1938 at a dance at Normy

Baths," she began to explain. "They'd just started boarding the pool over for the late autumn and winter months for dancing and such like, because there was nowhere else to go for it. I remember it well as it was my seventeenth birthday, and my Jack was eighteen, although he wasn't strictly *my* Jack – yet."

"Wow!" Jenny uttered, an almost disbelieving look on her face. "That's some memory."

"Not really," Elizabeth replied, matter-of-fact, "when you realise that that's the most important date in my life, along with having my baby boy – and that pales into insignificance now. Those four and three-quarter years were the happiest I've ever spent, and I've relived every second over and over ever since."

"You've never married?" Jenny asked, understanding well the difficulties of being a lone parent. "That must have been hard."

"No, I didn't feel the need," she began, confident in her answer. "I was bereft at losing him, but nobody else could have begun to fill his boots. He was the only one I ever wanted. He was called up in 1940, but before then, we had a wonderful time together wandering the highways and byways of Normanton and Altofts. He lived at 156 Church Lane, Normanton, and I lived at 150 Church Road, Altofts. You couldn't get closer than that, mentally and emotionally."

"Normanton Baths hold many good thoughts for me, too, both swimming and dancing," Jack said, memories floating in his eyes. "Mi fatha took me when I was six to teach me to swim. He picked me up, threw me in about halfway down so mi feet couldn't touch bottom, and shouted 'Now swim thissen out of that', and so I did – in a fashion."

"I remember the baths being opened in March 1926," Elizabeth continued. "March 26th. It was a Friday, so my mum told me."

"So, what must you have been then, Aunt Elizabeth?" Jack asked. "Five?"

"Aye," she replied, a smile touching her face briefly at this young man's perception and understanding. "Just about. Most o' t'money to build was donated by the miners – over £16,000 out of a total of more than £18,000. Not a huge amount by today's standards, but then it was a king's ransom. One of the councillors was dead against the idea, branding it an aberration and a mistake that would fail. He had his mouth well and truly closed when over two and a half thousand bodies went through t'turnstyle in the first week alone."

"Mi Mam told me a lot about mi Uncle Jack," he said, changing direction slightly, "but it came as a bit of a shock to find out he had a son. It was a bit of a capper also to realise that *you* are still here with us."

"What are you trying to say, Young Jack?" Elizabeth replied, a grin lightening her face.

"You know what I mean," he said, joining in with her gently poking fun.

"Your mam knew all about us, you know," Elizabeth explained. "She even encouraged us to rejoice in each other, because 'you never know what's around the next corner' she had said. No truer word was ever spoken, I'm afraid."

"You enjoyed your time together,"Jenny added quietly, "but sadly it was all too short."

"Ah, but," Elizabeth interrupted, "I don't think there was anywhere in this area that we didn't walk in those four wonderful years. We spent many a glorious hour in and around the Newlands Estate, the bluebell wood down Birkwood, wooden bridge over the canal and river at Stanley Ferry, the Ings at the end of Foxholes Lane in Altofts, and the walk over the fields and through the railway tunnel to Altofts from Ash Gap Lane. We made our own entertainment – and memories.”

She stopped talking suddenly as she dabbed at her eye corners with her lacy hanky to stop the glisten from becoming a deluge. She hadn’t spoken like this to anyone save Jack’s mam. Elizabeth’s son wasn’t interested in hearing about *her* memories, and it was such a joy to have her nephew there who found all her remembrances intensely fascinating and moving.

“You do me good, Our Jack,” she continued once she had regained control of her emotions, “and—”

“It’s good to remember and share emotions that have lain dormant for such a long time,” he interrupted, recognising those self-same feelings he shared with Jenny over his mam’s death and interment.

“You are *so* like your Uncle Jack,” she continued, “and your mam, of course. It’s uncanny how close you are to them both, even now.”

-o-

“You’re quiet,” Jenny said softly as they turned left at The Four Lane Ends at Whitwood, ready to grab the road to Leeds and home.

“Just thinking about what Aunt Elizabeth’s been saying,” he replied. “To think, if we hadn’t met Eric and Ellen, we would never have discovered this part of my family – a part I’ve been wanting desperately to find out about for years. Now I can fit into place a few more jig-saw pieces.

“Fancy your mam not only *knowing* them,” Jenny said, “but being party to their relationship.”

“I would still like to have seen them,” Jack replied, a threatening tear in both eye corners, “just once.”

Jenny looked at him as he concentrated on his driving. How could she ever consider, even for a second, living her life without this precious man – the man who gave everything for her and her children? She would not – could not - find anyone even close to his lovely – sometimes annoying – mind.

Would she be able to banish all thoughts of Simon from her mind for all time? She knew that the slightest suspicion she threw in Jack's direction would see her family rocked and ultimately destroyed.

She *had* to be strong, but…

Chapter 22

"Well, Ar Jack," Young Eric said, thumbs under trouser bracers and an impossibly jubilant look – for him – on his face, "tha's off to want to congratulate me, si thi."

"Oh aye?" Jack replied, standing next to him in front of his hearth, warming their backsides in time-honoured West Riding fashion. "And why might that be, then? And tha's not towd me yet where yon Ellen is."

"That's t' 'ole point, Brother," Eric said. "Tha's not gi'en me chance to tell thee."

"Well then," Jack urged him, "spit it out, man. I'll not know what tha's on abaht unless tha tells me."

"Tha's just become a uncle," Eric blurted out loudly. "This mornin', like. It's a lad. Eight pound nine ounce."

"Bugger me!" Jack gasped. "That's a big un and no mistake. Ellen all rayt?"

"Aye," Eric said, nodding seriously. "Rayt as ninepence."

"Well," Jack urged after a silent hiatus. "What's tha off to call him? Eric?"

"No bloody fear!" he insisted, a rueful grin underlining his decision emphatically. "Not decided yet. Well, Ellen's not decided yet. Onny one decision's clear. *Eric* is out o' t'question for 'is name."

Jack laughed as he slapped him on the back as a member of that elite group – Fathers Together.

"Ee 'ell," Eric went on, "it wor 'ard, tha knows. I wor sweating cobs when it wor ower."

"You were there? In the delivery room?" Jack said, a gasp heralding his surprise.

"I wor that!" Eric replied without hesitation or regret. "It wor an experience I'll niver forget – or replicate. It wor wonderful and awful at t'same time."

"Plannin' on 'aving any more nippers then, Our Eric?" Jack asked after a moment's pause. He didn't want Eric to think he was prying, but families tend to share such snippets, don't they – particularly close families.

"I don't know, si thi," Eric replied, unsure of the future. She says maybe and I says whatever *she* wants. Can't decide really. We'll atter wait and see, I suppose. I'd like one or two more, really. 'Appence a couple of lasses would sort yon lad out, I should imagine. Where's Jenny this evening?"

"Parents' evening drop-in, I think," he replied, "for our George. Jessie's on stop ower wi''er pal … Jessie, and Florence May is on another stay-ower wi''er Grandma Flo and Grandpa Jim. So, we've got the house to ourselves, for a bit anyway. Bottle of Guinness, cup of tea?"

"Aye," Eric agreed, "go on then."

They both laughed, comfortable in each other's company and with their shared history.

–o–

"Quick drink after the event?" he said, a smile creasing his face, hoping for a positive answer.

"Can't," Jenny replied, heart beating quickly at the thought of what might be, should she agree. "Got to take my son home and my husband will be waiting. Don't forget that I have a family to see to, and you … don't."

Should she arrange a clandestine meeting with Simon in the future? Should she give in to this overwhelming feeling she had been beset by several times already? Too dangerous. She knew the outcome should such a course become known, and she couldn't risk that. If she didn't, she would never know. Her man trusted her implicitly, and she knew *he* would never have such thoughts, such temptation. So, why had *she*? What was it? Was it the excitement such a dangerous move would bring, or was she ready for a change? The latter was out of the question because she would lose everything that mattered to her – everything she had always wanted and couldn't bear to lose. Was it the daredevil rashness of her late teens that had been resurrected by his attention, or was she rebelling inwardly about being in a rut?

The walk home with her son brought back the time when her husband had rescued her from a lifetime of loneliness and had brought back meaning into her life at a time when despair could have taken her. He had showered her with love, had adopted her illegitimate daughter as his own, and had given her two lovely children. How could she forget all that, and risk losing the life he had given her – all for a brief fling, a minor flirtation?

The simple answer was that she couldn't.

But, what if…

-o-

"And being our ambassador for junior French would provide the local authority with a well of first-rate teaching experience to draw from," Mr Atkinson eulogised. "It would also mean a substantial increase in both capitation for Broughton Junior School and in your salary."

"Sounds wonderfully almost too-good-to-be-true," Jack replied, a grin growing. "Yet what would it mean as far as my teaching is concerned? Would I have to move, for instance?"

"Of course not," the inspector assured him. "It would

mean only a few days out each year, to set up initiatives in other schools, to support those starting to teach French in *their* schools and to maintain the standards you would set for them. What do you say? Interested? It's all been agreed with your head teacher, by the way."

"May I think about it for a while, Mr Atkinson?" Jack asked, a thoughtful frown creasing his brow.

"Of course you may," Mr Atkinson replied. "Take as long as you need."

"OK," Jack said after a moment or two's thought, "I've made up my mind. Count me in."

"Capital!" the inspector grinned, getting to his feet to shake him by the hand. "Capital. I'll put in writing with terms and a remuneration package within a day or two. I'll have a word with Mr Aston on my way out."

Jack sat back in the staffroom almost overcome with the excitement of what he had just agreed to do, not quite sure whether he had made the right decision. The door jumped open as David bounced into the room.

"Well done, Jacky-boy!" he said, wringing his hand in congratulation and gratitude. "Signed, sealed and yet to be delivered."

"What have I just agreed to do, Old Chap?" Jack said, brow creased, and head tipped slightly to one side in his usual sign of puzzlement. "Signed my life away to the highest bidder?"

"What you've done. Old Man," he replied seriously, "is to guarantee the school's ability to move with the times, to keep us at the forefront of educational development, and – this is the big one for you – to ensure a big leap forward professionally for you, along with a huge boost to your wages. I *knew* we could rely on you. As it's Friday, what would you think to dinner at Gianni's in town, on me?"

"Gianni's?" Jack gasped. "But you can't get in there for love nor money. How do you propose to swing that one?

Courtesy of Littlewoods by any chance?"

"Courtesy of Gianni, actually," David assured him. "I used to teach his son, Aldo, when he was ten. Gianni's been grateful ever since. He always says I kept him on the straight and narrow and gave him the self-confidence and courage to pursue his professional ambition as a top-class chef."

"Then I accept, from the bottom of my stomach," Jack replied emphatically, with rolling eyes and a huge grin. "I'll need to phone Jenny to arrange for the children to be put out to servitude for the evening."

"I've already arranged for ours to be shackled by their Grandma," David chuckled, "so it should be a good evening. No car, by the way. You can now afford to travel in style by taxi. Six o'clock on the nose be OK?"

-o-

"Tell me those numbers again," Jenny urged her husband, as she sat on the edge of the lounge settee unable to drink her cup of tea because of her overwhelming excitement at his news, "and what it's going to mean for us as a family."

"A twenty per cent increase in salary to start with," Jack explained patiently, matter-of-fact, "which will allow us to have several holidays a year and boost our standard of living significantly. We'll be able to get a much bigger car, and second one for you, if you want."

This utter selflessness was one of the reasons she loved him. It was always 'we' and 'us' with Jack – never 'I' or 'me'. He always thought about his family first and foremost, and the effect any change would have on them.

"And does that mean you won't have to search for work anywhere else?" she ventured, fingers crossed in anticipation.

"At least for the time the scheme is in place," he assured her. "If it runs for at least a couple of years and *then* closes, they can't reduce my salary. So, being the pragmatic cynic I was born, that's as close to a guarantee for our financial future as you are about to get. I'll just have to wait for the contract's minute detail before I'll know for sure what it all entails, and, more importantly for us, when it starts. Consequently, don't go thinking you can spend it all – just yet."

They laughed easily, excitedly, as she hugged and kissed him.

"You're a clever man, Jack Ingles," she said with a sigh.

"Right place, right time," he said dismissively. "That's all."

"Is it going to mean more work for you, then?" Jenny asked, unable to contain her excitement and enthusiasm for what their new-found affluence could bring.

"No more than I do now, really," he replied, pouring a fresh mug of Yorkshire Tea to dunk his Hobnob in.

"Did you know…?" he went on, eying his biscuit.

"Yes, Jack I do know that a Hobnob will sustain five dunks in your tea without dissolving and collapsing into the cup to form a biscuit sludge at the bottom," she replied with a sigh. "Job? Extra work?"

"Oh, yes," he apologised, explaining how the new system was going to work, and how it would benefit everybody, not the least of whom were the Ingles.

"So, you see," he went on, thrusting his thumbs through imaginary trouser bracers, "this sort of stuff is what I was trained to do. Out of all the teachers in this authority already teaching French to junior nippers, they've chosen me to figurehead the move. A huge amount of confidence in my abilities, although out of those that already teach it, very few have been trained in method and rationale, like as what I have, Ern."

"You can take it, Big Man," she smiled with pride, ignoring his pathetic attempt at mimicking Eric

Morecambe. "Shoulders are wide enough, and despite your trying to minimise, they have chosen the right man. I love you for what you are doing for us. We all love you, don't we, Flo and George?"

The two children had just walked in from being with their respective friends.

"Yay!" they both cheered as they launched themselves at Jack, who wasn't quick enough to escape this human avalanche.

Chapter 23

"We're off to call t'lad James," Eric's deep voice crackled over the telephone, Sunday morning. "I've allus 'ad a fancy for t'name, and Ellen 'as a uncle called James. So that's what it's off to be."

"Excellent choice, Eric, Ar Kid," Jack replied, a great grin cracking his face. "When's t'christening? Any time soon?"

"Aye," Eric said, a note of pride and emotion etching his voice. "That's wor I wor phoning thee abaht, si thi. We wanted you and yon Jenny to be t'fust to know, like, along wi' Ar Joyce. I shall telephone 'er in a minute or so. We want to talk about t'christening when we see you."

"Champion," Jack enthused. "Is thy excited, then?"

"Too bloody rayt I am!" he replied, " Can't ger it aht o' mi 'ead. I've got a son as is t'image o'me, so they say. Niver 'ad one o'them afore, but then *thy'll* know 'ow it feels. I'll need one or two more to catch up wi 'thee."

Jack burst out laughing at his naïve but good sense of humour.

"And what does Ellen think on it?" Jack asked.

"Bloomin' eck!" he exclaimed. "*She* says she wants a 'ouse full, so I'd better get mi skates on, ant ah? Any road, we'd like you both and Joyce and Stick to come to ours on Saturday for a bite and a drink or two, ifn you've nowt better on."

"Eric, we'd love to," Jack replied excitedly. "There's niver owt better than seeing you two. Than noz that."

Their brotherly babble faded away good-humouredly. This was something he had never shared with William. Eric was a bit rough around the edges but highly intelligent and skilled in his chosen field, and polite and excited that he had discovered a brother and sister he thought he would never experience. He would have liked a relationship with the elder brother, but he was convinced he would never be able to share with William what he had with Jack and Joyce.

"Anybody interesting?" Jenny asked as she entered the room at the tail end of Jack's telephone conversation.

"Eric just phoned to invite us to theirs for a meal on Saturday," Jack replied. "He's invited Joyce and Stick so I thought we might share a car, so—"

"I was rather hoping to go to Mum's on Saturday," she interrupted quickly.

"Well, we can go there on Sunday, can't we?" he said, eyebrows raised in expectation.

"*I* was rather hoping to go to Mum's," she replied quietly, not looking him in the face.

Jack was quiet for a few stunned moments, not expecting *that* response at all. They had always done everything together, gone everywhere together, and now it was as if she didn't want to be with him. This thrust thoughts of her *almost* relationship with Simon to the forefront of his mind.

"Oh," he said slowly. "So, you've got something else on, on Saturday? Might I ask what, and why aren't I, your husband, invited?"

"I *can* change it to Sunday," she added, still without looking at him.

"You haven't answered my question," he insisted, a look of annoyance and suspicion creeping across his face. "Why do I get the distinct impression that you are involved with some clandestine thing that I am not party to? OK. If that's what turns you on, fine, but what happened to the relationship we had where we had no secrets from each other?"

The silence between and around them had become so tangibly oppressive and overwhelming that she didn't know how to respond, and she simply turned around and walked out.

He found her moments later in their bedroom, sitting on the couch with tears in her eyes.

"What is it, Jenny?" he asked quietly as he sat by her, sliding his arm around her shoulders. "What's happening to us? Is it something I've either said or done, or have you just stopped loving me like you used?"

Although it hurt her deeply to have the love of her life think this about her, she couldn't tell or involve him. A promise is a promise.

"OK," he said quickly, disappointment and sadness swimming in his eyes. "Can I take it that you will, at least, come on Saturday and take yourself off to your mother's on Sunday?"

"Yes, I will," she replied, lifting her head to him, "and I *do* love you, Jack."

"Yes, I know you do," he said, unconvinced, "but how much these days?"

She watched him get up and leave the room. She heard the click of his slippers disappearing down the stairs and along the hallway to the front door. As soon as she heard the snick of its Yale latch, she burst into tears.

-o-

"What is it with women, eh, Jack?" Stick Walker said as they boarded the X225 into Leeds City Centre the day after.

"How do you mean, Stick?" Jack queried, puzzled at the reference.

"Well," his friend went on, "Joyce asked me if I would like to go out to dinner on Saturday coming, and when I said I wasn't bothered, she stalked off in a huff and wouldn't say why."

"It's called being married, Our Stick," Jack replied, a rueful smile trying to make light. "It's to do with an invitation from our half-brother, Eric, who's invited the four of us over for a meal. Jenny's been funny about the whole thing, and at the mo, I'm the only one going."

"Make that three, Jack, now that I know what it's all about," Stick said, with a sigh of relief. "I thowt it wor summat I'd said."

They both chortled as they trouped off the bus in City Square.

"I'd know the back of *that* head anywhere," Jack shouted as they walked through the bus shelter onto the open pavement.

"Eh?" Stick said, not quite sure what was going on.

Jack walked smoothly over to an attractive young woman who was about to cross the road where Boar Lane shouldered its way into City Square.

"If it isn't Jane Alison Bradley," he said, touching her on the arm.

She spun around, a frown showing her annoyance at being stopped from crossing. As soon as she saw who had accosted her, she grinned and flung her arms about his neck. Stick's face betrayed his surprise at his friend's strange behaviour.

"Stick," he announced, "I should like you to meet Jane Alison Bradley, the Iron Maiden from the Steel City – the young lady that every man at college would have given ten years of his life to date."

"You always were a smooth flatterer, Jack Ingles," she

laughed. "Long time no see. You promised to write, but I suppose you said that to all your many admirers, eh Jack?"

"I heard you'd taken up wi' a young lad called Ian," Jack explained, "and so I couldn't queer someone else's pitch, could I, when he'd beaten me to it?"

"Ever the gentleman, eh Jack?" Jane said. "What brings you here?"

"We both work in Broughton," Jack added. "Just off to catch the Number 1 bus."

"Coincidence," she whooped. "Me too. Just got a job at Cross Farthing Street."

"Coincidence indeed," Jack said, clicking his fingers. "I'm at Broughton Junior and Stick's school is on Old Lane."

"Double Dutch," she laughed. "I only just know where *my* school is. So, shall we travel together? The Three Musketeers, eh?"

"Too right!" Jack said, a smile forcing out the frowns of earlier. "And we'll tell you where to get off."

They all laughed as they squeezed their way onto the almost full lower deck of the Number 1 Broughton special.

"She's lovely, Jack," Stick said, once she had left them at her stop. "A corker, in fact. Did you date her at college, then?"

"No such luck," he replied wistfully. "All the lads loved her, but she wasn't interested. Wanted to get on with her work and to do the best she could. Courting didn't form part of *that* plan, just then."

"Iron Maiden? Steel City?" Stick puzzled. "Although I think Iron Maiden is now a bit more ... obvious from what you said."

"Steel City?" Jack repeated. "She's a Yorkshire lass ... from Sheffield."

-o-

"That was a lovely meal." Stick said to Joyce on their way home. "Though I have no idea why Jack and Jenny decided to go in *their* car when we live so close."

"Did you notice a sort of strained atmosphere between them," she replied, "or was it my imagination?"

"Now you come to mention it," he replied with a grin, "no, I didn't. But then, I've never been susceptible to atmospheres – except for the one I'm breathing, Fortunately."

"Daft bugger," Joyce said, laughing at his naivety. "There's definitely something 'not right' with Our Jack. He seemed to be very happy and convivial, and his usual life and soul. Yet, I've known him almost as long as I've been on this earth, and something's not quite … right."

"As a nipper, Jack always was able to keep his feelings and emotions under wraps," she went on, "but he can't hide it all – not from me. He's had a lot of problems with his ex-wife, and I just hope it's not history repeating itself."

"Did I tell you that we met one of his ex-flames from his college days?" Stick ventured as they passed the library down Castleford Road.

"No," she replied. "When was that, then?"

"Two or three days ago," he said, "as we were heading for the Broughton bus to school, in City Square."

"Kept that quiet, Our Stick," she smiled. "Old flame? I didn't know he had any then."

"Well," he explained, "perhaps not strictly 'old flame'. Anyway, he knew her and they were on intimate hugging terms."

"Intimate? Our Jack?" she harrumphed. "You sure? Only, the last time I knew it, he didn't do intimate with anybody but Jenny. You certain?"

"Perhaps I was over-emphasising it a bit," Stick replied, more than a little embarrassed by his interpretation of what he saw. "She was very attractive, though."

"Gi' ower digging thi own grave, husband," Joyce advised, "or you might say summat you might regret. Still, point taken, because there is definitely *something* not right."

-o-

The cooler evening was welcome after an unseasonably warm day sitting in Ellen's oasis of a back garden. She was an astonishingly good cook who could have graced any professional kitchen, and her curried lamb with saffron rice *had* to be good to obtain the compliments that Jack lavished on her. Good, because this was the first time he had ever eaten it.

"Excellent day," he said as they headed for the front door. "Good news that Ellen is starting college and a new life in September, with James' christening on 9th August. Before we know it, 1980 will be saying 'hello' to 1981, and I will be thirty-five. Do you mind being married to an older man?"

"Older man?" she scoffed. "Just over a month older?"

"Cup of tea followed by love-making on the settee?" he suggested as he latched the door behind them. "Like we used to?"

"I'm tired," she replied, "and if you don't mind, I'd like to go to bed. Children are back tomorrow, and I promised I would go to Mum's."

"Just a thought," he sighed, not having made love to his wife for some time. She had always been 'busy'.

"You coming up?" she asked tentatively.

"I'll stay a bit," he replied. "A few things I want to think about ower a cup of Yorkshire, if you don't mind. I won't disturb you when I'm ready."

He noticed she hadn't either kissed him or wished him good night as they always used to do, and as he sat with his tea, his mind drifted back to Jane Bradley. She was a lovely woman and … No, it didn't do to dwell, and he had several urgent problems he had to consider.

-o-

Sunday turned out to be very fair, occasional flashes of sun glinting on the remains of the night-before's welcome showers. By the time he reached the breakfast table, Jenny was no longer there. On his table place mat, she had left a terse note that said simply – 'Gone to Mum's. See you later'.

Apart from her brief stays in hospital, this was the first time they hadn't breakfasted together, which both concerned and upset him. The children weren't due back from their various sleep-overs until late afternoon, so a stroll through Roundhay Park seemed like a capital idea. Just the place to settle his mind and blow off the cobwebs.

The bright green late spring foliage welcomed him into his usual strolling haunts, where scent-laden paths caressed his senses and drew him further into his therapeutically habitual walks.

Few strollers frequented the park at this time of day, particularly down by Waterloo Lake, not far from the glass house where he met Lee on her return from her mother's funeral in Canada. Two or three couples sauntered unhurriedly, enjoying each other's company as they rejoiced in late spring togetherness, rather like he did with Jenny in their early days in Normanton's Haw Hill Park.

He turned from his lakeside path and stopped mid-stride, as he took particular notice of a man and woman heading slowly towards the glass house on the rise, overlooking the lake. They smiled at each other contentedly, comfortable in each other's company, walking, arm in arm.

Jack froze, shrinking behind a large bed of dense

potentilla shrubs, in an attempt not to be seen. Now he understood. Blissfully unaware of Jack's presence, smiling happily as if she had not a care in the world, ambled his wife, arm linked with another man.

Jenny had found someone new.

Other titles from Frank English

All Right Jack is the fifth book in the series about Jack Ingles - a semi autobiography series:

Volume 1 Jack the Lad   *(2016)*
Volume 2 Jack   *(2016)*
Volume 3 Hit the Road Jack   *(2017)*
Volume 4 Welcome Back Jack   *(2017)*

Children's books:

Magic Parcel: The Awakening   *(June 2010)*
Magic Parcel: The Gathering Storm   *(March 2011)*
Magic Parcel: A New Dawn   *(August 2012)*
18 Mulberry Road   *(September 2011)*
25 Primrose Walk   *(January 2013)*
Autumn Adventures   *(September 2013)*
Winter Tales   *(September 2014*
Towards Spring   *(September 2016)*
Juniper's Tale   *(August 2018)*
Honey   *(January 2019)*
The Story of Lemuel Pecker   *(April 2019)*
Josephine's Journey   *(June 2019)*

Frank English

Born in 1946 in the West Riding of Yorkshire's coal fields around Wakefield, he attended grammar school, where he enjoyed sport rather more than academic work. After three years at teacher training college in Leeds, he became a teacher in 1967. He spent a lot of time during his teaching career entertaining children of all ages, a large part of which was through telling stories, and encouraging them  to escape into a world of imagination and wonder. Some of his most disturbed youngsters he found to be very talented poets, for example. He has always had a wicked sense of humour, which has blossomed only during the time he has spent with his wife, Denise. This sense of humour also allowed many youngsters to survive often difficult and brutalising home environments.

In 2006, he retired after forty years working in schools with young people who had significantly disrupted lives because of behaviour disorders and poor social adjustment, generally brought about through circumstances beyond their control. At the same time as moving from leafy lane suburban middle-class school teaching in Leeds to residential schooling for emotional and behavioural disturbance in the early 1990s, changed family circumstance provided the spur to achieve ambitions. Supported by his wife, Denise, he achieved a Master of Education degree in his mid-forties and a PhD at the age of fifty-six, because he had always wanted to do so.

Now enjoying glorious retirement, he spends as much time as life will allow writing, reading and travelling.